Scott Flynn.

I knew Scott Flynn.

He and Jackson had been friends.

I'd had a crush on Scott for as long as I could remember.

I had gotten over that crush, of course, after I left home for college.

I hadn't seen him since and I hadn't heard anything about him. It was odd seeing his name here. Maybe it wasn't even the same Scott Flynn.

As I stood there contemplating the odds of it being the Scott Flynn I knew. Or not. The door opened and Scott Flynn stood there looking at me.

I saw recognition flit across his expression.

He had the same strong jawbone that I remembered with the addition of a five o'clock shadow that gave him a look far more grown-up than the teenager I remembered.

Everything about him was grown-up. He was no longer the tall, spindly teenager I had crushed on. He was tall and lean now.

Dark hair in a stylish cut brushed the top of his collared shirt.

His eyes held a mix of curiosity and amusement.

"Bianca?" His voice was deeper than I remembered but still familiar.

My heart fluttered sending my blood racing through my veins.

I completely forgot why I was standing here. All I could think was how very odd it was that he staying here at the lodge.

Perhaps I hadn't quite gotten over that crush so much as I had thought.

Christmas Wishes

ALPINE FALLS

KATHRYN KALEIGH

Christmas in Alpine Falls

(Reading Order)

Stranded in Alpine Falls

Belonging in Alpine Falls

The Spirit of Christmas in Alpine Falls

Christmas Wishes in Alpine Falls

Finding True North in Alpine Falls

A Ghost of Christmas Magic in Alpine Falls

All of the books in the Alpine Falls Series standalone and can be read out of order. However, some books have characters from the previous stories in them.

Contemporary

(Reading Order by series)

(VOWS OF INHERITANCE SERIES)

Vow to Protect

Vow to Redeem

(ALPINE FALLS SERIES)

Secrets and Second Chances

Honeymoon with a Stranger

Not Our Wedding

Stranded in Alpine Falls

Belonging in Alpine Falls

The Spirit of Christmas in Alpine Falls

Christmas Wishes in Alpine Falls

Finding True North in Alpine Falls

A Ghost of Christmas Magic in Alpine Falls

(SILVER PINES SERIES)

The Way Back to You

Back to Where We Began

When We Were Us

(ONCE UPON FOREVER SERIES)

My Forever Guy

Our Forever Love

Forever Vows

Finding Forever

Accidentally Forever

(TRUE NORTH SERIES)

Borrowed Until Monday

Still Mine

The Moon and the Stars at Christmas

Perfectly Mismatched

On the Way to Forever

A Merry Little Christmas

On the Way Home to Christmas

It was Always You

(UNBREAK MY HEART SERIES)

Begin Again

Love Again

Falling Again

(FOR THE LOVE OF THE FLIGHT SERIES)

Just Stay

Just Chance

Just Believe

Just Us

Just Once

Just Happened

Just Maybe

Just Pretend

Just Because

(MAGNETIC NORTH SERIES)

Second Chance Kisses

Second Chance Secrets

First Time Charm

Three Broken Rules

Second Chance Destiny

Unexpected Vows

(FALLING FOR CHRISTMAS SERIES)

The Heart of Christmas

The Magic of Christmas

In a One Horse Open Sleigh

A Secret Royal Christmas

An Old Fashioned Christmas

(CITY SKYLINE BILLIONAIRES SERIES)

Billionaire's Unexpected Landing

Billionaire's Accidental Girlfriend

Billionaire's Fallen Angel

Billionaire's Secret Crush

Billionaire's Barefoot Bride

(TRULY, MADLY, DEEPLY SERIES)

The Lady in the Red Dress

On the Edge of Chance

Sealed with a Kiss

Kiss Me at Midnight

The Heart Knows

(STOLEN ECHOES SERIES)

When Cupid's Arrow Strikes

Chasing Fireflies

A Chance Encounter

(EDGE OF THE HORIZON SERIES)

The Forever Equation

Pretend Boyfriend

All our Tomorrows

Kissing for Keeps

Out of the Blue

The Princess and the Playboy

(RED LIPSTICK KISSES SERIES)

Red Lipstick Kisses and Small Town Wishes

Stolen Dances and Big City Chances

Chance Connections and Upside Down Plans

A Christmas Kiss on the Twenty-Fifth

Believe in the Magic of Christmas

All of the books in each Series are standalone and can be read out of order. However, some books have characters from the previous stories in them.

ROMANTASY

(IN THE SPIRIT OF LOVE)

Spirits of the Heart

Out of Dreams and Ashes

Etched Upon the Heart

WESTERN ROMANCE

(LONE STAR HEARTS)

Wanted by a Texas Ranger

Saved by a Texas Ranger

(WHISKEY SPRINGS)

Finding Natalie

Promising Samantha

Falling for Allyson

Saving Savannah

Claiming Charlie

Rescuing Keira

Protecting Gabriella

Courting Isabella

TIME TRAVEL

(INTO THE MIST)

Written in the Wind

Scripted in the Stars

Destined in the Twilight

Promised in the Mist

Trapped in the Melody

(DRAGON'S BLOOD)

Dragon's Blood

Lavender Blue

Champagne Silver

Twilight Frost

Mountbatten Pink

(WHEN HEARTSTRINGS BECKON)

Rescued in Time

Meet me in 1879

(WHEN HEARTSTRINGS ECHO)

Messages Across Time

Falling Through to Forever

Once Upon a Winter's Spell

(BECKONED)

Before the Storm

Twist of Fate

When the Stars Align

Once Upon a Christmas

Once in a Blue Moon

A Wish Upon a Star

(BEGUILED)

When Lightning Strikes

Storm of Time

Midnight Storm

When the Moon Falls

Stormborn Angel

(SPELLED)

Time Tempest

The Heart Remembers

A Moment in Time

Moonlight Shadows

HISTORICAL

(TAPESTRY OF BLUE AND GRAY)

Shadows Beneath Magnolia Blooms

Secrets Among Southern Roses

(IT HAPPENED BY ACCIDENT)

Accidentally Alluring

Accidentally Married

(SOUTHERN BELLE CIVIL WAR)

Beyond Enemy Lines

Love Always

Hearts Under Siege

Hearts Under Fire

Away Down South in Dixie

The Reluctant Bride

Stay with Me

Jasmine Kisses

Magnolia Kisses

Gardenia Kisses

(THE QUINNS)

Wait for Me

Take Me Home

Keep Me Safe

FATED MATES

Riley's Mate

Aiden's Mate

Brayden's Mate

STANDALONE SUSPENSE

Lost and Found

All I Want for Christmas

Serenity

Courting Alley Cat

*Sign up for my NEWSLETTER to get all my romance releases, sales, Kickstarter announcements, and a **FREE** romance, SEALED WITH A KISS*

Christmas Wishes

One

Bianca Flynn

"That's it," I said, snapping off the decade old projector plugged into my laptop. "Does anyone have any questions?"

The room seemed quieter without the steady hum of the projector.

I blinked at the sudden brightness after flipping on the overhead lights and went back to stand behind my podium. I picked up my to-go cup of coffee, then set it back down.

One of the more vocal students sitting on the first row of the small auditorium raised his hand.

"Yes Marcus?"

"Will the final exam be open book?"

I made a face and several students laughed. I walked out from behind the podium and looked around at the students. They were scattered, but not crowded, from the front row to the very back row. It held over two hundred, but this only had an enrollment of seventy-one. A small auditorium. Ten rows of twelve on either side of the middle aisle. A little dated, but great acoustics. It was my favorite room to teach in.

That and this had been a good class. Every class was different. Psychology 101 was a good class to begin with and this had had good interactions.

"Can anyone answer this question for Marcus?"

About twenty students, half the class, raised their hands. I pointed to a girl in the back who never spoke up. The last day of class was better than never.

"Alicia," I said.

"No," Alicia answered.

"No." I repeated to Marcus who just shrugged. I guess he had to try one more time. "Take some time. Study. We've gone over everything that will be on the test."

Students quietly closed their computers and slid them into their backpacks. A few students closed their paper notebooks.

"My graduate assistant will be administering the test," I said. "So I'll see some of you in January for Psychology 102. Merry Christmas everyone."

Right on cue, the bell rang officially declaring the class over.

The bell, unnecessary as it was, shattered any semblance of quietness. I went back behind the podium and closed down my own equipment. Packed up my laptop computer.

I took a sip of my coffee, but it was cold, so I set it aside to toss on the way out.

Alicia came up to stand next to me. She held her textbook against herself like a shield.

I smiled at her. Alicia was one of my best students, even though she was quiet. Her brown eyes were deep, making me think of the saying "still waters run deep."

"Dr. Flynn." Alicia shifted her backpack. "I just wanted to tell you that I really enjoyed your class."

"Thank you Alicia. You're graduating soon, right?" Alicia was a business major who had come to psychology late.

"In the spring."

"Have you decided on what's next?"

"Graduate school," she said. "I want to do what you do."

"You want to be a professor?"

"Yes! That's what I'm thinking."

"Have you started applying to graduate schools yet?"

"Not yet." She shifted her feet and looked down.

"It's okay. You've got plenty of time. Do some research on graduate schools over the break, then come talk to me when we get back in January."

"I will. Thank you."

"Load up on psychology courses for the spring. That will help."

"Yes ma'am."

"Don't worry. I'll help you."

But right now, I needed to get out of here and get on the road.

I wanted to get to Alpine Falls tonight.

Walking down the hallway, I sent a text to my boyfriend Bradley.

> Are we still on track to be ready to leave by one o'clock? We can get lunch if you're ready by Noon.

I stepped into my office and gathered up everything I needed to take with me. I already had everything packed up and ready to go.

My textbooks. I was old-fashioned and liked to hold an actual book in my hands. I wasn't sure I knew how to read a book without a highlighter in my hand. I might not have much time for lecture prep while I was home, but I should have at least a little.

My little succulent. It didn't need much water, but I was going to be gone for a whole month and that was too long to leave it unattended.

My laptop was already packed, so after I slid my textbooks into my leather book bag, I was pretty much ready to go.

I took one last look around at my little office. Bookshelves lined with books on one wall. A big wooden desk that I liked to keep cleaned off. Nothing but my desk top computer and keyboard.

I didn't have much of a view. My window, about three feet by three feet, looked out over the parking lot four floors down.

I put on my black wool coat with its soft faux fur collar. An early Christmas gift from Bradley. It was good for Denver, but I was going to need my heavier quilted coat when I got to Alpine Falls.

My hometown of Alpine Falls was at just under ten thousand feet, framed on three sides by tall rugged mountain peaks. It was so high in elevation it wasn't uncommon for the town to be closed off from snow.

It was especially beautiful at Christmastime. I could never wait to spend my month long holiday break with my family.

I liked living in Denver. I like the energy that came from the urban environment. The shopping. The restaurants. The culture.

But Alpine Falls was home and I would always have a special affinity for it.

Just as I was about to leave, I got a response from Bradley.

BRADLEY

I got tied up. You go ahead. I'll meet you there.

I scowled at the text. Read it again.

Bradley and I had been planning this trip for two months. We'd only been dating since September, but our relationship seemed solid almost from the beginning.

> Wait. You aren't coming?

BRADLEY

> I'm sorry, Babe. I got tied up with a client. I'll call you later.

Bradley, clinical psychologist, worked at the mental hospital downtown.

He got tied up sometimes. It went with the territory.

But today?

Why today?

My car was packed. I was ready to go.

And he was supposed to go with me.

We'd been planning it.

He was going to meet my parents and I was going to show him around Alpine Falls where I had grown up.

I took a deep breath.

> Do you want me to wait for you?

I didn't want to wait for him, but it was what a good girlfriend was supposed to ask.

BRADLEY

> No. You go ahead. I'll catch up.

> Okay.

There. I had at least asked. I didn't like it that he wouldn't be making the drive with me, but I would have liked it less if I'd had to wait for him.

I'd already made arrangements to leave the university early. To have my graduate assistant administer my final exams.

I was on my way.

Two

Scott Brooks

I lowered the wheels on the little Cessna and prepared to take the airplane in for a landing.

The runway barely qualified as a runway, but it was better than driving in on winding backroads, especially when the evening would be turning dark shortly.

Since the Alpine Falls runway had no lights, I couldn't land here at night.

I had, however, managed to come in just at sunset.

Even though the mountain peaks were capped with snow, the skies were clear. The sun, hovering at the edge of the horizon, ready to drop, splashed pinks and red across the sky.

I always thought of sunsets as nature's paintings. Fleeting, but beautiful.

A quick check of the instrument panel told me that I was in good shape to take the airplane in for a landing.

It had been ten years since I had been to Alpine Falls.

It was a long time to go without visiting my hometown, but my parents had sold our house while I was in college and moved to Arizona to get out of the cold.

That only left my grandfather living in Alpine Falls.

Since he traveled to Arizona for the holidays, I'd had no need to come back here.

Until now.

Now I was tasked with doing something with Grandpa's house.

He'd moved in with my parents and something had to be done about his house. It couldn't just sit empty.

My mother refused to leave Grandpa and my father refused to leave my mother, hence I had been elected.

So I had a plan. I would take care of whatever needed to be done at the house, then fly down to Arizona to spend Christmas with my family.

Noah Worthington had given me a leave of absence to take care of these things. He was all about family.

Family first, he said. That was the philosophy he lived by.

After my wheels touched down in a smooth landing, I taxied off the runway out of the way and proceeded to go through my post flight checklist.

The airplane belonged to Noah Worthington of Skye Travels. Noah was a self-made billionaire who had started his company with one little Cessna airplane, smaller than this one, and grew it into an empire with a fleet of airplanes.

Skye Travels was the company where newly graduated pilots lined up for jobs.

Noah was very selective in who he hired and all things being equal, he hired family first.

I was fortunate to have gotten hired on five years ago.

Like everyone who worked for Noah Worthington, I was loyal to him. I couldn't imagine working for anyone else.

If I did anything, I wanted to go out on my own just as Noah had and work for myself.

Fortunately, I was realistic enough to know that Noah worked harder than anyone else possibly could, myself included, and he'd had timing and not a little bit of luck on his side.

It took all those things to have the success he had.

It also helped that he now had a big family and they all did their part. It was unbelievable how he had grown his company while he was growing his family.

As soon as I opened the airplane door, I recognized the familiar feel of Alpine Falls.

The light clean air that smelled like spruce and pine. The sound of the river with its rocky bed in the distance. So different from the sluggish rivers that looked like murky ponds in Houston where I lived now.

By comparison, Alpine River was barely a little stream.

But here it was considered a river. I don't know why the town was called Alpine Falls. No one knew. There were no waterfalls nearby. At least not now. Maybe there had been falls back when the town was named.

Maybe. Maybe not.

I stood beside my airplane and realized just how long I had been gone from here.

I had just landed what was basically out in the middle of nowhere, unless I counted Alpine Lodge and the Flynn manor house. The runway was on Flynn property, but Noah's assistant, Maggie, had cleared my landing.

There were no Ubers in Alpine Falls and no complimentary cars for pilots.

Well. I had most definitely been transformed into a city boy.

Even if Maggie hadn't realized that I needed to arrange transportation, I should have.

With no other options, I set off on foot to the lodge. From there I could walk into town. It wasn't that far. It was just that somehow arranging transportation hadn't occurred to me. Since Maggie always handled things like that, I wasn't beating myself up about it.

But... there was one thing.

I had hoped to avoid Alpine Lodge on this trip.

The path from the airfield took me straight to Alpine Lodge and I went in through the back doors.

Since I wasn't a guest here, I wasn't comfortable going in through the front doors. The valet and doorman would ask and rightly so for an explanation. A man on foot with no luggage.

I just needed to grab a bottle of water from the lounge or maybe the gift shop and be on my way.

I'd spent my share of time here in the lodge as the best friend of Jackson Flynn, son of the owners of Alpine Lodge. Like most high school boys, we had played some, but the Flynns ran a tight ship and visiting Jackson had often come with a cost.

When I was here with Jackson, we had to work. Mostly we had to muck out the two fireplaces and add fresh hewn wood. It wasn't bad, all in all, but we spent most of our time at my house where we were free to play video games and eat pizza without interruption.

My parents, professionals who drove into Glenwood Springs to work every day, were rarely home leaving me and my sister pretty much on our own.

Walking into Alpine Lodge was a bit surreal. It hadn't changed one bit.

The large four-sided fireplace in the middle of the lobby still burned real wood and people still sat around it. The was one difference though. Instead of holding books, they read on their devices. Phones and iPads.

I didn't see a single person out of half a dozen holding a real printed book.

That, at least, told me I hadn't stepped back in time. Good to know.

I didn't recognize the girl at the front desk and I was too far away to read her name tag.

I decided to hit the lounge instead of the gift shop.

Sitting down for a minute, having a beer, was sounding like a good idea.

I had no idea what I was walking into at Grandpa's house. For all I knew, there wasn't even any power on.

The hostess, I didn't recognize her either, seated me at a booth near the front of the lounge.

Now that I thought about it, I had not planned this trip very well.

First of all, I didn't have a vehicle. My luggage was still in the airplane.

And assuming the worst, I didn't have a place to stay.

I ordered a beer and checked my messages. Just my mother checking to see if I had landed.

> Do you know if there is power on at Grandpa's house?

MOTHER
> Let me ask him.

My beer arrived and I took a sip from the refreshingly cold bottle.

My first beer at Alpine Lodge.

MOTHER
> He doesn't know.

> How can he not know?

MOTHER
> He isn't himself.

Maybe I didn't want to go to Arizona after all. If

Grandpa was getting dementia, I didn't want to see him like that.

> It's okay. I'll go over there and find out.

MOTHER

Where are you?

> At the lodge.

Mother. Let me know what you find out.

I took another sip of beer.

So that was how it was going to be.

My mother was leaving this situation up here in Alpine Falls to me.

I guess she had her hands full down there with Grandpa.

MOTHER

I just called the utility company. They said the power was turned off due to not being paid.

Great. So I had that on my shoulders. It was my responsibility.

MOTHER

Are you at the Lodge?

> Yes.

MOTHER

Maybe you can stay there.

And the lodge could be at capacity. If they didn't have a room, I didn't have a whole lot of options. I could fly into Denver. Get a room there and come back in the morning.

I glanced at my watch. If I was going to go, I needed to do it quick.

Leaving some bills on the table, I went out to the front desk.

The girl's name was Zoe.

"Hello Zoe," I said. "Do you happen to have a room for tonight?"

"Oh. Let me check before I say no."

Exactly what I figured.

Someone really needed to put a hotel in Alpine Falls.

While Zoe checked her computer, I checked my weather app.

Below freezing tonight. There was no way I was going to be staying in Grandpa's house without electricity.

"It must be your lucky day," Zoe said. "We just had a cancellation."

I wasn't sure just how lucky my day was going, but at least I'd have a place to stay tonight.

Three

Bianca

One of the things I loved about home was that it didn't change. At least not much.

The employees changed from time to time. There was a new girl behind the front desk.

But the valet and the doorman were the same.

The front desk, like the rest of the lodge was tastefully decorated for Christmas. A potted poinsettia sat on one side of the desk and two more sat on the floor in front of the desk.

A cork board with crisscrossed elastic bands displayed greeting cards from friends and guests.

My sister-in-law ran the gift shop now, replacing Gertie who still came to work now and then, but Gertie, after working here for as long as I could remember, was no longer a fixture here.

My favorite part of the lodge was the big fireplace right in the center of the lobby. It was an architectural marvel. Open on all four sides.

There was a smaller, regular sized fireplace in the lounge/café, but between the two of them it took a lot of firewood to keep them going. A lot of work, too.

My brothers had often been expected to keep the fires going and after they left home and my sister, Arabella, took over the lodge, she had to hire high school boys to do the job.

Since it was little more than a week before Christmas, the tree was already up and fully decorated. I had fond memories of spending an afternoon every year decorating the tree with my family.

Every year, my father and brothers made a trek out on our property and came back dragging a very large blue spruce tree. Somehow the trees always looked pretty much the same.

Thanks to my great-grandfather's foresight, we had a never-ending supply of blue spruce Christmas trees growing on three acres of our property. He'd planted the trees in orderly rows and they thrived. It was hardly even noticeable that we cut one down every year, especially since we planted another one in its place.

The tree, tall enough to reach the top of the wide

stairway leading to the second floor, was decorated with a mix of old and new decorations and everything in between. The old wooden garland that had belonged to my grandparents and maybe even their parents before them was draped around the tree along with clear, twinkling lights.

It was decorated with lots of balls and other ornaments, a lot of them gifts from guests. It had recently become kind of a thing for guests to bring a decoration, usually something representing where they came from, with them and hang it on the tree.

We had decorations from as far away as Charleston, South Carolina.

With oversized wrapped faux gifts in silver and red beneath the tree, it had become a popular photo background.

I'd stopped by the house—there was no one home—changed out of my work clothes into jeans and a sweatshirt, then headed over to the lodge.

My sister Arabella was there. As the manager, she was always either walking around taking care of one thing or another or holed up in her office, working on scheduling. At least she had finally given up sitting at the front desk taking care of reservations.

I found her in her office.

"Hey," I said.

"Hey. You're here early." She looked over my shoulder. "Where's...?" She frowned.

"Bradley."

"Right. Where's Bradley?"

"Detained. He'll be up later."

"Huh." She shrugged. "Okay."

"Where are Mom and Dad? I didn't see them at home."

"Christopher flew them down to Denver to do some shopping."

"You're kidding, right?"

"No. Why?"

Arabella rarely kidded about anything. She had, however, gotten a whole lot more relaxed since she'd gotten married to James. But there was no hint of a smile on her face at the moment.

"No reason. Except that I just drove from there." Arabella just looked at me. "I could have used a ride on the helicopter."

"You always drive," Arabella said. "I didn't think you liked flying."

"That's not really the point." But she was right. I wasn't all that fond of flying. And to be fair, no one had known I would be coming up before next week. I hadn't told anyone I'd gotten off before finals.

"Are you busy?" Arabella asked, moving along to what she considered a more pertinent topic.

"Not exactly at this moment," I said warily. "Why?"

"Want to help me?"

"That depends. Do I have to muck out the fireplace?"

"You know that's not the right word."

I grinned. "It's what we call it."

By we I meant my younger siblings and me. Jackson had

called it mucking out the fireplaces one day and since we hated cleaning out the fireplaces, the name had stuck.

Our parents, whether by design or accident, no one knew and they had never said, had given birth to their children in two sets of three.

There were the older three. Christopher, Arabella, and Reed. All just a year between them.

Then there were the three younger ones. Me. Jackson. And Drew. All just a year between us, too.

But there was a decade separating the two groups of us, so essentially our parents had raised two different families.

All three of my older brothers, including Jackson, had become pilots.

Arabella had gotten a business degree and returned back here to run the lodge.

I had become a college professor. About as far from mucking out fireplaces as a person could get, in my opinion.

Maybe I'd done it unconsciously. Maybe not so much.

I loved my family and I loved Alpine Falls, but I did not love mucking out fireplaces.

Arabella held up a stack of papers.

"I need to put these flyers under the guests doors," she said. "No mucking involved." She emphasized the work *mucking,* obviously not amused.

"Sure," I said. "I can do it."

"I have them divided by hallway. I can do half."

"I'll do all of them," I said, holding out my hands. "It'll keep me from having to do anything else for awhile."

"You do realize we have a *family* business," Arabella said, crossly. "Right?"

I just grinned at her and taking the flyers, headed for the stairs.

Arabella organized activities every year for those guests who came for the Christmas holidays. The activities culminated in a Christmas Eve masquerade ball that had become quite an event over the years.

And every year she slid what she considered official, but informal, invitations beneath their doors.

As I walked up the wide stairway, I imagined as I always did when I used these stairs, what the lodge must have looked like when it was first built over a hundred years ago.

I imagined it must have been filled with elegantly dressed men and women who came here for a destination holiday much as they did now. My sister was responsible for bringing that element of sophistication and destination back to the lodge with her masquerade ball.

There were people who came every year and spent as much as two weeks at the lodge.

Most of those guests were well off, but not so well off that they had their own vacation homes.

Our guests could drive in, fly in, or take the train that came in directly from Denver. Relatively speaking, the train was new.

Altogether the three options gave us a nice variety of guests.

Reaching the top of the stairs, I stopped to read the

numbers on the folded flyers. She had guest names and room numbers, hand written, on each one.

Following the numbers, I turned right first and began sliding the folded flyers under the doors.

When I reached the last door at the end of the hallway, I stopped and stared at the name.

Scott Flynn.

I knew Scott Flynn.

He and Jackson had been friends.

I'd had a crush on Scott for as long as I could remember.

I had gotten over that crush, of course, after I left home for college.

I hadn't seen him since and I hadn't heard anything about him. It was odd seeing his name here. Maybe it wasn't even the same Scott Flynn.

As I stood there contemplating the odds of it being the Scott Flynn I knew. Or not. The door opened and Scott Flynn stood there looking at me.

I saw recognition flit across his expression.

He had the same strong jawbone that I remembered with the addition of a five o'clock shadow that gave him a look far more grown-up than the teenager I remembered.

Everything about him was grown-up. He was no longer the tall, spindly teenager I had crushed on. He was tall and lean now.

Dark hair in a stylish cut brushed the top of his collared shirt.

His eyes held a mix of curiosity and amusement.

"Bianca?" His voice was deeper than I remembered but still familiar.

My heart fluttered sending my blood racing through my veins.

I completely forgot why I was standing here. All I could think was how very odd it was that he staying here at the lodge.

Perhaps I hadn't quite gotten over that crush so much as I had thought.

Four

Scott

From my room at the lodge, I had a spectacular view of the rugged Rocky Mountain peaks. I was always impressed that Alpine Falls was so high in elevation and yet it was surrounded by jagged mountain peaks that scraped the sky on three sides.

By my calculations, I had about thirty minutes to get back to my airplane, grab my luggage, and walk back before it was full on dark.

After freshening up, I left my leather book bag on the bed, grabbed my keys and headed back out.

The first thing I noticed when I opened the door was the candles glowing in the sconces along the hallway.

The second thing I noticed, maybe even at the same time, was the girl standing at my door.

I recognized her immediately even though it had been a full ten years since I had seen her.

Bianca Flynn.

Jackson's little sister.

Dark hair, flowing over her shoulders.

Sparkling green eyes the color of emeralds. Except that Jackson's eyes were blue, the two of them had the same eyes. She looked at me with wide eyes framed with dark lashes.

Her red bow-shaped lips were slightly parted in confusion. She looked as confused as I felt right now.

Even though she had never seemed to have any interest in me and being the teenage boy that I was, I hadn't been particularly interested in girls back then. Jackson and I had been far too busy playing video games and football and anything outside.

Even though I hadn't been all that interested in girls, Bianca had always been the one I would have been interested in if that had been different.

And if I'd thought about her a few times over the years, well, I was a red-blood American boy. What could I say?

I'd often had to catch myself to keep from staring at her. And now, although she had been pretty as a teenager, she had grown into a beautiful young lady.

And here she was standing at my door. Almost like I had conjured her up.

"Bianca?"

"Scott? What are you doing here?"

"I just got into town." I was, quite honestly, surprised that she remembered me, much less recognized me.

"Me too," she said.

I glanced at the stack of folded papers in her hands.

"Invitations," she said, following my gaze.

"Invitations?"

She handed me one with my name on it.

I looked from it to her. I hadn't been here long enough to warrant anything with my name on it.

"I just got here," I pointed out.

"Arabella," she said as though that explained everything. And, truly, it did.

"I'll look at it later," I said, suddenly remembering my mission. "I have to get to the airport."

She took a step aside. "Are you leaving?"

"What? No. I have to get my luggage." I closed my door behind me.

"We can send for it," she said.

"That's not necessary," I said with a little smile. "I can be there and back in no time."

"Okay."

I stopped and turned around. "It's good to see you," I said.

"You too."

I left her standing there as I headed toward the stairs.

The candles in the sconces flickered as I passed even though they were behind glass globes that kept any breeze from blowing them out.

Nothing that happened at Alpine Lodge surprised me. I

shrugged it off and kept going. So many possible explanations.

I needed to get my luggage from the airplane before dark, but I also needed to give some thought to unexpectedly running into Bianca.

I hadn't been avoiding her, not exactly. I just hadn't been expecting to see her. I especially hadn't been expecting to see her standing outside my door.

Jackson and I had drifted apart after high school, but like guys tended to do, I still considered him a friend. If I were to run into him right now, we could pick up our friendship as though we'd just seen each other yesterday.

Probably wouldn't play video games though. Maybe a game of pool or maybe just sit and have a beer.

At any rate, since Jackson and I were for all intents and purposes still friends, there was a guy code that dictated I not date his sister.

Or rather there used to be a code. Probably another reason I hadn't done anything more than look at Bianca. A boy would've had to be blind not to want to look at her.

Was the guy code still a thing or had that changed in the last ten years? I hadn't heard anyone talk about it. Maybe it wasn't even an adult thing.

I had to do some research on that before I made a fool out of myself.

Bianca was the kind of girl that had a man worrying about things like guys codes when he was supposed to be worried about what the hell he was going to do about his grandfather's abandoned house.

Retracing my steps out the back door, I headed down the path toward the airfield.

I wasn't going to make it there and back before dark.

Fortunately, someone had installed some solar lights along the path to light the way.

Well. That was a welcomed improvement.

I passed the fork in the path. Going right would take me to the Flynn's home. Going left took me to the airfield.

Either way was canopied with a mix of blue spruce trees, maple trees, and aspens that had already shed their golden leaves.

As I neared the airfield, I saw a sleek little Phenom sitting near the runway.

The airplane would belong to Reed Flynn.

The helipad had been there when we were kids, but the runway, though still barely a runway by city standards, was vastly improved.

All in all, it was strange being back in Alpine Falls.

The last time I had been here, I had been driving the little pickup truck my family had bought for me.

I'd come a long way since then.

But being here, with no vehicle at all, I didn't feel like I'd come all that far.

And seeing Bianca, well... I felt like I was a boy again.

Five

Bianca

I finished distributing the invitations and headed back downstairs.

I did not, however, go back in the direction of my sister's office. She was as bad, if not worse, than our parents had even been about putting us to work.

Since I'd just put in a full week's work at the university and had driven in from Denver, I wasn't feeling up to putting in an evening's work at the lodge.

No offense to the family business.

Instead, I went to the lounge in search of something to eat.

The lodge itself was, as always, quiet. People didn't

come here to stay in a lodge at ten thousand feet to be forced to listen to music. Instead, it was one of their options.

The lodge offered them quietness.

Quietness that included that crackle of the fireplace. The crickets. The howling of wolves outside.

But the lounge was a different story.

Café by day. Lounge by night.

In the evenings, like now, music spilled from hidden speakers. Christmas music at the moment since the lodge was all about Christmas during the month of December.

I took a seat in a booth toward the back and the server brought me a sparkling water.

The booth was nestled up against a wall of windows that looked out over the lobby.

I had no messages. No word from Bradley. I thought about texting him. Asking him how everything was going, but I held back.

The ball was in his court. And I was still mad at him for ditching me the way he had. So he could just wonder if I'd made it.

We pretty much did our own thing. Went out every week. This visit here was a big step for us.

I ordered a burger and fries and while I waited, I watched the lobby.

I would have been lying if I'd said I wasn't looking for Scott.

My brother's friend in high school, just one year older than me, Scott had never shown any interest in me.

Sometimes I'd catch him looking at me, but I'd always quickly looked away and so had he.

He and I had never had a conversation. Jackson had always been there and with such a big family, it would have been impossible for us to have ended up with a moment alone. Not that we would have known what to say to each other if we had.

The last I'd heard, Scott had become a pilot. Go figure. Just like Jackson.

They had taken their love of video games and transformed that love into flying airplanes.

Jackson had followed in our older brothers' footsteps. It made sense that Scott had done the same.

Scott came from a small family. Just a sister. So it made sense that he had followed my brothers into aviation.

But hadn't his family moved away?

To my knowledge Scott hadn't been back since going away to college.

I sipped my sparkling water and tried to remember any pieces of conversation I might have overheard about him over the years.

Anytime anyone mentioned Scott's name, I had listened.

But I'd never come right out and asked about him.

I suppose I'd been afraid that if I did, they would have been able to see right through me. To see that I was crushing on my brother's friend.

The server moved aside after setting my burger and fries on the table and there he was.

Scott Brooks.

He was looking right at me.

I actually glanced over my shoulder to see if there was someone behind me that he might have recognized.

But no one behind me was paying Scott any attention.

And now Scott was headed in my direction.

I straightened, the food in front of me all but forgotten.

"Hi," he said.

"Hi."

"There's a line to get a table," he said.

I hadn't even noticed that the lounge had filled since I'd sat down. I'd been lost in my own thoughts.

As he looked at me questioningly, it occurred to me that I should ask him to join me.

"You can sit here," I said.

"Thank you."

As he sat down across from me, I saw the easy confidence in him that went along with being an airplane pilot. I should know. I had three brothers who were pilots and each and every one of them could be insufferable at times.

Something about being a pilot made them cocky.

Scott wasn't looking cocky. Or insufferable. But he was looking confident. Nothing wrong with looking confident.

"Did you get your luggage?" I asked.

"I did. Someone's done some work on the airfield."

"My father and Noah Worthington."

"Noah?"

"Yeah. Skye Travels leased the airport, I think. I don't know the details."

"How did I not know that?" he asked.

"Should you have known it?"

"Considering that I work for Skye Travels, yes. But I don't know much about Noah's business."

"Huh." How did I not know that Scott worked for Skye Travels? "Reed worked for Noah for some time."

"I know."

"It seems we're all part of one small world."

He settled back against the booth, looking quite relaxed.

The server came and asked if he wanted anything.

"I'll have what she's having," he said, then turned back to me. "Actually it's not all that surprising."

"What's that?"

"That we've all worked for Skye Travels at some point."

"Jackson never mentioned you," I said.

"We don't see each other," he said easily. "He still works out of the Denver office?"

"He does."

The server brought Scott's plate and set it down on the table in front of him.

"Can I get either of you anything else?" the server asked.

I shook my head. Considering that my food was cold now.

"I think we're all good," Scott said.

Then he quite simply traded plates with me.

Just like we ate together all the time and it was nothing at all.

Six

Scott

"You don't have to do that," Bianca said.

"Do what?" I asked, already dipping a fry—from what had been her plate an instant ago—into some ketchup.

"Change plates," she said.

"It's my fault yours got cold," I said. "But if you aren't going to eat, then my sacrifice will have been for nothing."

She studied me carefully as though trying to figure me out—if she could do that, she was doing better than most—then picked up the hamburger in front of her and took a bite into it.

I smiled to myself.

Even though I'd eaten with Bianca's family a hundred times, I'd never had dinner with Bianca.

Maybe I'd gone about making it happen in a slightly devious manner. But who could fault me?

I wasn't the same clueless teenager I'd been ten years ago. I'd learned a thing or two.

I'd seen a pretty girl, a girl I'd known practically all my life, eating alone. It would have rude to have done anything other than join her.

Unlike most places out west, Alpine Falls was known for their hospitality. I think that was one of the reasons I loved Houston so much. It was like an urban version of Alpine Falls.

A place where it was not only okay to be a gentleman, but was expected.

"I heard you're a college professor," I said.

"How did you hear that?" she asked.

"It's a small town."

"But you haven't been back in ten years." She bit her lip as though she had just realized that she had given away the fact that she had kept up with me.

I smiled. "I still hear things."

She seemed to think it was best to let that go.

"So what are you doing here now?"

I much preferred talking about her to talking about the work I had ahead of me.

"My grandfather," I said.

"Right. Is he okay?"

"He moved to Arizona with my parents and left his

house here. It seems I've been designated to do something with it."

"He just abandoned it?"

"I don't think he could handle it anymore. His health isn't all that great."

"I'm so sorry." She leaned forward and looked at me with genuine sympathy in her green eyes.

"Yeah. Me too. But my mother's taking care of him."

"Are you headed there, to Arizona, for Christmas?"

"After I get Grandpa's house taken care of."

"What are you going to do with it?"

"Check out the condition. Get an estimate. See if my mother wants to sell it. Do you want to buy a house in Alpine Falls?"

"No thank you," she said without hesitation. "I'm quite content in my Denver condo."

"I have an apartment in Houston. What with never being home and all." I felt the need to explain to her why I was nearly thirty and still living in an apartment. Normally it didn't bother me.

"Makes sense. I spend a lot of time at home."

"My cousin is a college professor. She works ALL the time. Lectures. Tests. Papers."

"Lecture prep is the worst," Bianca said. "As professors, we have to actually read the textbooks."

"Imagine that." Amused, I smiled.

I'd watched Bianca from afar for a very long time.

Getting to actually talk to her was even better than I had imagined it would be.

Seven

Bianca

The Christmas music spilling from the hidden speakers in the lounge changed to a classic song, one with a catchy tune to it. It was a little hard to hear at times due to the lively conversation coming from a table across from us.

The noisy table had a loud family. Two adults and two teenagers. One younger child about ten-years-old. They reminded me a bit of my family, only smaller.

Scott and I talked companionably while we ate.

I felt a little bad that he was eating my slightly cold food, but at the same time I found it completely charming and besides, he didn't seem to mind in the least.

I lost track of time as we talked. I could see why Scott

and my brother were such good friends. Scott was funny and kind. And smart.

I'd known these things, of course, but actually having a conversation with him was unexpectedly... well... nice.

"I wondered where you got off to," my older sister Arabella said, coming up to our table. "Hey Scott."

"Hey."

"I got all the invitations delivered," I said before she could ask.

"Good. But that's not why I'm here."

Couldn't my sister see that I was having dinner? And not just dinner, but dinner with Scott?

It was like she didn't even bat an eye seeing us together.

What was ground-shaking to me was noneventful for my sister.

I would have to think about that later.

Right now my sister was about to put me to work. I could see it in her eyes.

"What do you need?" I asked.

She pulled a key out of her pocket and laid it on the table.

"Actually it's a job for both of you."

Scott and I exchanged a glance.

"There is a crib in the attic. I need you to go get it."

"No," I said, shaking my head. "I'm not going up there. It's dark."

"Why is a crib in the attic?" Scott asked.

"We needed it out of the way and that was the most logical place to put it at the time."

"Makes sense," Scott said.

Did they not hear me say I wasn't going up there?

"You can hold the door for him," Arabella said.

"I'm not—"

But she was already walking off, leaving the key on the table.

"Something's wrong with Arabella," I said.

"Why do you say that?" Scott asked. "I don't mind going up to get it."

"It's dark," I said.

"There should be lights, right?"

"That's not the point." I lowered my voice with a quick glance around to make sure no one was listening. "We can't go up there at night."

"Why. Dr. Flynn," Scott said with exaggerated astonishment. "Are you afraid?"

"I'm not— Maybe."

"Well I'm not." He picked up the key. "Like she said you can hold the door. Unless..."

I rolled my eyes at him. "I can't let you go by yourself."

"You could, but that is a very good answer."

I took a drink of my sparkling water and pushed my plate aside. I was finished eating anyway. So why not?

I glanced at my watch. It wasn't even seven o'clock yet.

"We'll be fine," I said out loud to myself.

"I just have to pay," Scott said, looking over his shoulder for our server.

"Don't worry about that. Arabella can pick up the tab."

Expecting him to follow, I left the booth and headed out of the lounge.

Stepping into the lobby and walking toward the stairs, it was markedly more quiet.

Scott fell into step beside me and walking with him was markedly surreal.

He was only a year older than me, but he'd always seemed older than that. Not only older, but he seemed to always know what I was up to. Not in a weird way, but in a way that told me he paid attention.

Like now. He somehow knew I was a college professor and had my Ph.D. I hadn't told him that and as far as I knew he and Jackson didn't talk. And even if they did, I couldn't imagine them talking about me. They wouldn't have any reason to.

And yet he knew.

Half a dozen people sat in the comfortable chairs around the four-sided oversized fireplace in the lobby. It did look inviting. Maybe I'd bring one of textbooks here and sit by the fire to read it. It would make reading and highlighting my new personality textbook a little less tedious.

The Christmas tree near the stairway twinkling with clear lights was packed with decorations.

An older couple stood in front of it having their photo taken by the valet.

That was how the staff at Alpine Lodge was. Always ready to step in and lend a hand whether it was part of their job description or not.

I glanced over at Scott.

He didn't even work here and he was lending a hand. My sister Arabella was that way. She could get anybody to do just about anything.

Her world revolved around the lodge—and James—and it showed. She worked tirelessly at keeping everything running smoothly.

Our parents had made the right move in naming her manager. They barely had to do anything anymore. Like today. Going shopping in Denver for the day. Something they never could have done before Arabella took over running the lodge.

It still stung a little that no one had asked if I needed a ride, but it was true, I liked having my car here and I wasn't overly fond of flying.

An odd trait for a girl who came from a family of pilots.

We reached the top of the stairs and turned right. The door to the attic was at the end of the hallway.

The candles in the sconces had burned down and it was almost time for someone to come up and blow out the candles. We never left them burning overnight. Safety hazard.

Personally I didn't see how leaving them burning in the daytime was any safer, but it wasn't my decision. Fortunately. I didn't want the responsibility for decisions like that on my head.

I'd always loved the lodge. It was part of my family's heritage. But being proud of where I'd come from was different from wanting to have a hand in running it.

I hadn't known what I wanted to do when I started

college. It was my second semester, sitting in a Psychology 101 classroom. The first day of class. That I knew. It hit me with clear certainty.

I wanted to be a college professor. In psychology.

And I had never once wavered from that conviction since that day.

My family was a little baffled, but they'd never been anything other than supportive about my decision. I'm sure they would have preferred that I live here in Alpine Falls, but it wasn't like any of them to quash a person's ambitions.

"Sometimes the candles seem to flicker," Scott mentioned as we walked down the long hallway.

"They do, don't they?" I looked at him sideways. I bit my lip to keep from pointing out that I had warned him that coming up here at night wasn't a good idea.

But I didn't do it. I didn't say a word.

The main reason I didn't say anything was because if he didn't know why, I didn't want to explain it.

Reaching the door, he unlocked it and held it open while I walked through, taking the first step up the narrow stairway.

Even down here, I could already smell a difference in the air.

The attic was stale and smelled... well... old.

The lodge was old, but it didn't smell old. The lodge smelled like beeswax. A little like honey and wildflowers.

But not the attic. The attic smelled musty and earthy and damp. I never understood how the attic could smell damp.

There was no dampness in Alpine Lodge. Even after it rained, the ground was dry again almost immediately. Unless it snowed. That was different.

But the attic.

The attic was a strange place.

As a scientist, I wanted an explanation. But there was no explanation.

My solution was to avoid it.

But no.

Arabella insisted we go up here.

I took a deep breath, squared my shoulders and went up the stairs, Scott's footsteps echoing mine right behind me.

Eight

Scott

Being from Alpine Falls, I'd heard the rumors.

But they were just rumors as far as anyone knew.

However. Being the best friend of Jackson, a Flynn, I knew that there was more to the rumors than just idle speculation.

I knew that it was generally accepted by the Flynn family that Alpine Lodge had a ghostly resident.

Her name was Abigail.

It wasn't that anyone ever talked about her. Not outright, anyway.

Now and then someone would mention that something

inexplicable had happened. Something that was benign but had no explanation.

Like candles flickering. Behind a glass.

And then moments later someone would whisper Abigail's name.

It wasn't hard to put to the two together.

Personally, I'd never had an encounter with Abigail.

It didn't mean I discounted her presence in any way. It just meant I hadn't had an encounter with her.

I wasn't afraid of something I had no reason to be afraid of.

Besides, I wasn't complaining about getting to spend some time with Bianca.

What was to complain about?

She was everything I remembered and so much more. She was the grownup version of the girl I would have wanted to date if I had dated in high school.

It just so happened that my group, namely Jackson and I, didn't date. We didn't go to dances or prom or anything like that.

Looking back, I didn't understand us. Looking back, all I could see was missed opportunities.

I wasn't, however, one to cry over spilled milk. I was a look forward kind of guy.

And if looking forward meant bringing along a girl from my past, then I saw no reason not to pursue it.

Reaching the top of the stairs, we stepped into a large attic. It was probably as large as the lobby below, but it looked bigger because it was just one open room with discarded items scattered around.

Bianca flipped on a light switch.

Further investigation told me that despite the random appearance, there was actually an order to it all.

Boxes marked Christmas Decorations were all together. Old trunks were in their own section.

The only thing scattered randomly was furniture, most of it covered with white sheets.

The white sheets were the eeriest part of the attic as far as I was concerned.

I lifted one of the sheets and peeked at a large sofa beneath.

"How did they get this up here?" I wondered.

"I don't know," Bianca said. "Let's just get this crib and get out of here."

We found the crib, an antique that had the heaviness that went with its age, and slid it over toward the top of the stairs.

"I think it's too big to get down these stairs," I said, gauging the looks of the narrow stairway.

"It has to," Bianca said. "They brought it up here. If they brought it up here, it has to go back down."

"You would think so," I said. Bianca was looking decidedly uncomfortable. She looked past me as though she expected to see a ghost at any minute.

"Okay. Let's give it a go."

"Yes. Let's."

"I'll go first. Keep it from sliding down. You just guide it."

Getting in front of it, I slid it to the opening of the stairway.

"This is a bad idea," Bianca said behind me.

I got the crib to the doorway, but it wasn't going.

"It's too wide," I said.

"Just turn it over on its side," Bianca said behind me.

"That won't work. It's taller than it is wide."

"We'll just have to leave it here," Bianca said, obviously quite okay with that.

"We can't do that."

"Any suggestions?" She started tugging it back away from the doorway.

"Let me do that. You're gonna hurt yourself."

She stepped aside and I got the crib out of the way and studied it a moment.

"We have to take it apart," I decided.

"How?" Bianca asked, putting a hand on the side of the crib.

"I don't know." I knelt down and looked beneath it. "It comes apart," I said.

"Arabella could have told us that."

"Maybe she didn't know." I stood up and dusted my hands.

"Maybe."

"I have to go down and get a screwdriver. You want to wait here?"

"Absolutely not," she said.

To make herself perfectly clear on that, she started down the stairs ahead of me. I smiled to myself.

This was turning out to be a most entertaining evening after all.

Nine

Bianca

It was Arabella's fault, I decided, for sending us up here. She could have sent one of my brothers. Christopher was the handyman, but since he'd flown our parents into Denver he wasn't available.

As for Reed, he could be anywhere. Probably at home with Bailey.

I wondered why she didn't ask James. Apparently he wasn't available either.

We wasted no time going back down the long hallway and down the stairs.

As we neared the front desk, I immediately felt guilty about my suggestion to abandon the crib.

A father stood there swaying a fussy infant. The mother sat in a chair someone had brought out.

Scott leaned over and whispered so only I could hear. "Feeling a bit guilty now, huh?"

"No comment," Bianca said. I followed her into a storage room where we found a tool kit.

"Do you want to take the whole kit?" she asked.

"Nope," I said, holding up a flat-head screwdriver. "I have what I need."

"Are you sure?" she asked, looking at all the different sized screwdrivers. "You only glanced at it."

"I know my way around some tools," I said.

"Right. Being a pilot and all."

Detecting a bit of sarcasm, I looked at her, but she just batted her long dark lashes at me with an innocent little smile.

That was all it took. I was sunk.

I'd already been right there on the edge anyway. That flirty little look sent me just right on over the edge.

"Okay," I said. "Let's not keep those parents waiting any longer."

"Yes. Let's don't."

We retraced our steps. This time I didn't detect any flickering candles.

Bianca knelt down with me and watched as I unscrewed the railings that had prevented the crib from fitting through the narrow stairway.

"What can I do?" she asked.

"You," I said. "get to hold these." I dropped a handful of screws in her palm.

Our palms touched just a moment, but it was enough to have me thinking about how soft her skin was. How delicate she was.

She wrapped her hand around the screws and took a step back.

"We'll take the rails down first," I said, not even bothering to tease her about staying in the attic by herself.

"Okay. I've got the door."

Carrying the two rails, I followed her down the stairs, leaned the rails against the wall, then we went right back up again. The crib was still heavy, but much more manageable without the rails attached.

With the screws held tightly in one hand, Bianca held the door with the other.

"I'll find out which room they're in and we can take it straight there."

Bianca pulled out her phone sent a quick text.

A response came back almost immediately.

"They're on the other end of the hallway," she said.

"Imagine that," I said.

She just smiled at me.

Ten

Bianca

The bellhop opened the young couple's room for us and I, doing my assigned job, held the door while Scott carried the rails, then the crib inside.

I was rather impressed at just how adept he was at not only taking the crib apart, but putting it back together.

He tested it, making sure it was all back together before we left the room.

We met the young parents on the stairs on our way back down.

"It's all good to go," Scott told them. "Enjoy your stay."

"You're a natural at this," I told him after the couple was out of earshot.

"I practically grew up here, too, you know."

"Yes. I suppose you did."

As we walked across the lobby, I examined that thought to see if it seemed weird. It did not. In fact, it seemed rather right.

I rather liked it that Scott had a shared history with me.

I liked it that he understood the importance of hospitality at the lodge.

And that he knew his way around.

"I wonder what Arabella will have us do next, "I said after we returned the screwdriver to the supply room.

"There is no telling," he said. "But..."

He looked over at me as we stood at the door to the supply room.

"I have an idea."

"What's that?" I don't think any girl could fault me for the way my heart raced a little faster.

"We can duck out back and take a moonlight stroll."

"We don't have our coats," I said, feeling compelled to lodge a protest, even though taking a moonlight stroll seemed like a splendid idea.

"You wanna wait here while I get them?" He asked with a glint in his eyes.

"I would, but." I stopped, realizing he was taunting me.

His coat would be in his room and my coat would be at the back door.

"Why don't we just meet at the back door?" I asked.

He grinned. "Good idea." He raised a hand to give me a high-five. "We make a good team."

I placed my hand against his, but instead of the intended quick slap of agreement, our hands lingered together for a moment longer than the requisite expectation.

Our eyes met and also lingered.

I cleared my throat. "See you at the back door."

We went our separate ways. He went upstairs to get his coat while I headed to the back door for my own coat.

As I slid into my wool coat, I wondered just how much trouble I was about to get myself into.

I pulled on my gloves and slid on my wool hat to keep the wind out of my ears.

It didn't really matter.

It didn't matter because I couldn't come up with a single scenario in which I did not agree to take a moonlight stroll with Scott Brooks.

As I waited for him to come back down, I wondered if there had been any research on just why a crush made early in life became an indelible part of our psyche.

I'd look it up when I got back to my computer. See if there were any studies on it in the literature.

In the meantime, I adjusted my gloves. Stopped to adjust my hat in front of the mirror near the back door.

My cheeks were slightly flushed and we hadn't even been outside in the cold yet. I swiped some lips gloss over my lips and decided that was better.

I turned just in time to see Scott, also bundled in his coat, striding toward me.

My heart fluttered and I couldn't stop myself from smiling.

How could a girl, any girl, not want to take moonlight stroll with Scott?

He opened the door and we stepped outside into the brisk night air.

The moon was full, reflecting off the snow-capped mountain peaks that surrounded us on three sides.

We automatically started down the path that led toward the river.

"I forget how bright the stars are out here," he said as we left the lights of the lodge.

Walking among the blue spruces, maples, and aspen trees, the only light guiding our way came from the solar lights that lined the path.

A wolf howled somewhere in the distance.

"Me too," I said. "I don't normally come outside at night even when I'm here."

"You shouldn't," he said without a hitch.

I didn't bother to tell him that wild animals didn't discriminate when it came to attacking people whether male or female.

I only wanted to enjoy the moment.

And besides I was feeling inordinately safe walking along beside Scott.

It was, after all, a moonlight stroll. And a moonlight stroll was romantic by definition. There was just no way around it.

Especially when the moonlight stroll was with Scott Brooks.

Maybe I had imagined taking a walk with Scott back

when we lived here, but never once would I have imagined it actually happening ten years later.

We reached the riverbank and left the path to stand at the edge of the river to watch the water flowing along the shallow river bed, tumbling over the rocks, with the loud roar that came along with the rushing mountain stream.

"I've been wondering about something," he said, standing close enough for me to hear him over the roar of the water.

My heart skittered. Had Scott brought me out here because he'd been wanting to ask me something? Maybe the romantic part of the moonlight stroll was all in my imagination.

Eleven

Scott

We stood close enough to the river bank that the dampness of the flowing water brushed against my face. When the wind turned just right, that dampness turned into fine little water droplets.

I hadn't had an agenda when I'd brought Bianca outside. I'd just known that I wanted to be near her. And I'd wanted to be alone with her.

But standing here at the edge of the river cocooned in our own little world surrounded by noise from the river and light from the moon, I felt compelled to explore possibilities with her.

"What have you been wondering?" she asked, tipping her head up to look at me. Her cheeks were flushed from the cold and her eyes bright.

We wouldn't stay outside much longer. The cold was energizing for a few minutes, but it didn't take long before it would become uncomfortable.

"I should probably ask Jackson, but he's not here," I said.

"What is it?" she asked. "You can ask me anything."

I got the sense that I was hearing a hint of the psychologist in her. It fit her well. She'd always been kind and understanding. In fact, I'd never heard her say a cross word with anyone.

"I've heard people... someone... say that there's a code about a guy not dating his best friend's sister."

She bit back a laugh. "What kind of code is that?"

"I don't know. I just always wondered if it was true."

"It sounds a bit silly to me," she said. "In fact, it's a bit counterintuitive. I mean. You already know the guy's family, so you don't have to deal with that. So why wouldn't you date her?"

"Good point," I said. "I guess if things didn't work out, it could cause a rift between the two friends."

"Guys have some weird ideas sometimes," she said, shifting her gaze to the river. "I wouldn't listen to them. If you don't take a chance, then how would you ever know if she was the right one for you?"

"I wouldn't know."

"See. Some silly guy rule. Just ignore it." She looked back at me.

"Okay," I said. "I will."

I lowered my head and kissed her. A chaste kiss, but right on the lips.

Straightening a little, I smiled at her.

She blinked at me, her eyes wide.

"You meant me," she said, the words coming out as a whisper.

I laughed out loud. I couldn't help it.

"Yes. I meant you."

"Oh." She pressed her fingertips to her lips.

"You thought I was talking about someone else?"

"I just assumed so," she said, sweeping a strand of hair out of her face.

"Does it change your answer?"

She tilted her head to the side and looked charmingly confused.

"Do you stand by your statement that a guy shouldn't date his best friend's sister?"

"Yes," she said. "But... I don't think it's a good idea for *us* to date."

I put a hand against my heart.

"Just one kiss and you're already breaking my heart."

She put a gloved hand on my arm. "You're silly."

She was probably right. I was silly.

But seeing her again, being with her, kissing her, told me that my teenager fascination, never explored, had merely lain dormant for ten years.

Sometime between then and now I had changed my philosophy on dating.

I might not have had much interest when I was a teenager, but now, as an adult, I had a whole lot of interest.

Especially in the girl standing in front of me.

Twelve

Bianca

The air coming off the river was a few minutes away from becoming uncomfortably cold.

"You're shivering," Scott said, linking his arm with mine and turning our backs to the river. "Do you want to go home or do you want to go back to the lodge?"

"I don't have any reason to go back to the lodge tonight," I said. "Arabella would just give us another task."

"I'll walk you home then."

It was a good idea. He was right. I was shivering even though I was bundled up. Living in the city, I didn't spend a lot of time outside.

Getting back on the path, we continued toward the house I would always think of as home and turned right at the fork. The left fork led to the airfield.

An owl called out, asking for our identities.

"I don't hear that in Houston," Scott said.

"Denver either. At least not where I live."

"You like living in the city?"

My arm was still linked with his and even though we were both bundled in our thick coats, I could feel the strength of his arm against mine.

"Sure. I stay busy. Working mostly."

Right now I was channeling my seventeen-year-old self and wondering how my life could have been different if I had taken a moonlight stroll with Scott back then.

Would I have walked with him if he'd asked? Let him kiss me?

I couldn't imagine him asking any more than I could imagine me not being willing to take a walk with him.

Even back in high school when he and my brother had been video geeks, he'd been cute. Not the handsome man he was now, but definitely cute enough that he could have dated any girl he'd wanted to.

He would have been the one breaking hearts if he'd simply decided to.

I looked over at him and wondered what kind of man he had turned out to be.

He seemed kind and funny and charming.

But now he had me wondering if he dated. I couldn't

imagine that he didn't. Even if he didn't set out to date, girls would hit on him. I was certain of it.

But he wasn't a geek anymore. A geek wouldn't take a girl out for a stroll and boldly kiss her in the moonlight with the river spray dampening their skin.

"What about you?" I asked. "Do you like living in the city?"

"I don't really care so much about the city as long as I get to fly airplanes. I can't say I spend a lot of time on the ground."

"You sound like Jackson."

"Not surprising. What about Christopher and Reed? They're pilots, too."

"Yeah." I shrugged as the lights of my childhood home, the Flynn Manor, came into view. "But now that they're married, they don't seem to have that same narrow focus."

"They like being home with their wives."

"So it seems."

"That must be confusing for them," he said.

"Confusing how?" I glanced over to see if he was kidding with me, but he wore a serious expression.

"Well. A pilot has a one-track mind. Flying. Girls come second."

"Until they don't," I said, nudging him playfully.

"And when they don't, a pilot has to figure out how to shift priorities."

"I don't think Christopher or Reed had any trouble shifting their priorities."

"Good to know," he said.

"Are you talking in hypotheticals again?" I asked. "It's okay if you are. I'd just like to know ahead of time."

"I'm just trying to figure out what I have to look forward to," he said with a little grin shot in my direction.

He was unabashedly flirting with me. And I was enjoying every second.

Thirteen

Scott

I slowed my pace as we neared the Flynn Manor.

The bottom floor windows were dark, but lights glowed in several of the second-story windows, suggesting that people had scattered upstairs to their respective rooms.

I'd spent my share of time in and around the big rambling house. The house. The lodge.

Jackson and I had escaped to my house to play video games and eat pizza, but I'd still spent a lot of time here.

That was a long time ago, but it looked almost exactly the same.

The house was well over a hundred years old. From what I understood, it had started out as a somewhat normal-sized house, but each generation had added onto it and now it just rambled. Wings, one-story and two-short, even a three-story suite, shooting off in various directions.

It had only one kitchen and dining area, but the rest of the house was made up of suites. There was room enough that a large family could live comfortably without stepping on each other's toes.

And that is just what they did. At one point three generations had lived in the house and no one thought anything of it.

I often envied them. The continuity of it.

My parents had sold their house, one they had built themselves, and moved to Arizona. And now I was charged with doing the same with my grandfather's house.

We had no long history of being in one place like the Flynn's had.

There was something grounded about it. Stable. Knowing that one family could live in the same house and run the same business—the lodge—for hundreds of years.

It just took one child to continue the traditions.

With the current generation of Flynns, that child was Arabella. She was the pivotal person in her generation. The one who would pass the heritage to the next generation.

Christopher and Reed would probably have something to do with it, too, but it wasn't their main focus. They, like me, were pilots. And that meant that their attention was divided.

It didn't mean, however, that they couldn't have children who carried on the tradition.

Probably would.

Already, Christopher's wife ran the lodge's gift shop. So even though Christopher was off flying his helicopter, his wife was making her place at the lodge.

Bianca and Jackson were the two children, so far, who had moved away and had nothing to do with the lodge. Nothing directly anyway.

And yet they still came home. They still had that connection that pulled at them. That was something I didn't have and never would have with my family.

Even if I wanted to, I couldn't. It wasn't part of who my family was.

"You look deep in thought," Bianca said as we started up the stairs leading to the front porch.

Three oversized wooden rocking chairs, old but sturdy sat on either side of the front doors. Potted plants, well-tended, sat here and there.

"It's just a little odd seeing the house again after all these years," I said, running a gloved hand over my chin. "It's like stepping back in time."

"I feel that way pretty much every time I come home," she said taking in the front porch. "There's always something different though. Like those plants. I don't even know what kind of plant they are."

"Something that thrives in the cold, I would think," I said.

"No doubt. Sometimes I wonder about how anyone has time for things like plants. I mean. My days are so filled, I wouldn't have time to do anything with plants if I wanted to, or even learn about them."

"You're busy."

"I'm busy," she said. "That's true. But I don't think that's it. Not all of it anyway." She shook her head and shivered a little. "Anyway. I need to get inside. Thanks for walking me home."

"Anytime," I said. "It was my pleasure."

She keyed a code into the keypad and opened the door. Turned the doorknob.

She took a step forward and I knew that our evening was over.

Pausing, she looked over her shoulder and gave me a little smile.

"Good night," she said.

"Good night."

I waited while she went inside. Locked the door.

Then I took a deep breath and slowly let it out.

Wow. Just wow.

The house and lodge might look pretty much the same way they had when I was a teenager, but I was not the same person.

And Bianca was certainly even more delightful than I had dreamed possible.

Fourteen

Bianca

Safely inside my childhood home, I leaned against the front door and pulled my coat more tightly around me.

After taking a minute to stop shivering from the cold, I pulled off my gloves and shoved them in my coat pockets.

I came home every single year for Christmas. In fact I had never missed a single Christmas here in all the years I'd been living away from home.

But things had changed. My three oldest siblings had gotten married, expanding our already large family.

Jackson, my brother just a year older than me, had moved away, too, but he never missed coming home for Christmas either.

He'd be here. He might fly in at the last minute, maybe even on Christmas Eve, but he'd be here.

I'd never brought a boyfriend home with me.

Until this year.

This time I was bringing Bradley.

Bradley.

I hadn't thought about Bradley all evening.

Pushing away from the door, I pulled my phone out of my pocket and checked for messages.

Nothing.

Nothing from Bradley. The guy who was supposed to be coming home with me today.

As I walked back to the kitchen for a glass of water, it occurred to me that Bradley didn't even have my parents' address.

Well. I took a glass from the cabinet and filled it with water.

That could be a problem.

Had it been my idea for him to meet me here or had it been his?

Now that I thought about it, he had rather brushed me off.

I should probably call him.

Or at least text him.

Wouldn't a good girlfriend at least check on her boyfriend?

I went to the back door and stared outside at the way the moonlight reflected on the snow-capped mountain peaks.

It was so beautiful here. Sometimes when was outside

walking or driving in Denver I'd catch myself gazing west toward the mountains and I'd feel a twinge of homesickness.

But I stayed busy and I didn't have time to dwell.

Had Bradley and I defined our relationship?

We'd been dating for several months, but we'd never really come right out and declared that we had an exclusive relationship.

I had just sort of made some assumptions.

I refilled my water glass and took it upstairs with me to my room.

I knew better than to make assumptions. I was a psychologist for God's sake.

As I unpacked, something I hadn't done yet, I wondered what it said about me that I had kissed Scott. Technically he had kissed me, but really, wasn't it the same thing?

I hadn't even thought about that until now.

It just seemed so natural.

But I couldn't let it happen again. Not while I was in a relationship with Bradley.

And even though I knew that I was right about that, it left me feeling a deep sadness that went all the way through me.

I'd had a crush on Scott since I was a teenager.

Tonight had been like a teenage wish come true. More than that. The teenage wish had a vague, unformed longing. Tonight had been a real moment between two adults who liked each other.

How was I supposed to just let that go?

How could I let it go when Scott was right here? Taking

me for a walk along the river and stealing a kiss in the moonlight.

My grownup self might be telling me I should be thinking about Bradley, but my teenager self, the part of me that was closest to my heart sighed with the memory of Scott's kiss in the moonlight.

Fifteen

Scott

Taking the familiar path back to the lodge, I breathed in the strong scent of the blue spruce trees, the pine trees, the scent of the chilly air that held the promise of snow.

Alpine Falls hadn't had its first snowfall of the season yet. Uncharacteristically late.

But it was in the air. I could feel it. Smell it.

It would snow before Christmas. Less than two weeks away.

As I walked back, the night sounds, a howling wolf, the flutter of a bird, I remembered why I was here. That I was here to figure out what to do about my grandfather's house.

I hated that it had fallen to me. Maybe not the final decision, but certainly looking for options and making a recommendation. My mother had her hands full taking care of Grandpa and Father did whatever Father did.

It was how it always had been with them. Not my idea of how a marriage should work, but then I'd grown up watching Mr. and Mrs. Flynn together. Watching my friend's parents, I'd formed my own opinion of what a marriage was supposed to look like.

Everybody was different but I'd chosen to model my expectations after Mr. and Mrs. Flynn.

I wanted a marriage like Mr. and Mrs. Flynn had. One where they did things together. Even just today, they'd gone into Denver shopping together.

Since I hadn't heard the chopper come back, I had to guess they'd ended up spending the night in Denver.

Slipping in through the back door of the lodge, I headed across the lobby to the stairs.

I'd get up early. Walk into town and check out the state of my grandfather's house.

Then I'd have a better idea what I was dealing with.

I passed the oversized four-sided fireplace in the middle of the lobby. Comfortable chairs on all four sides, most of them taken with people relaxing with their reading devices. One person actually reading a hardcover book.

I hadn't been much of a reader until after I went to work at Skye Travels. The founder and owner, Noah Worthington, was a firm believer that the hours upon hours of waiting that were built into the job of being a pilot, was best spent reading books.

To back it up, he was always sending us book recommendations and leaving books lying around the office.

Electronic games and mindless Internet scrolling, he insisted, were a waste of time.

I didn't dare tell him how much time Jackson Flynn and I had spent playing video games growing up.

I also didn't tell him that I attributed a lot of my piloting ability to skills I'd learned playing video games.

But I listened to him.

I'd taken up reading during those long hours of waiting.

Arabella was behind the front desk talking to a guest.

She'd always been an overachiever. That did not seem to have changed. I hadn't seen her husband, but it was my understanding that he, too, was a pilot, so he could be on a flight.

The Christmas tree, a tall blue spruce that towered up to the second floor twinkled with elegant clear lights.

They'd taken the old angel down, probably put her in safekeeping somewhere and put a new angel on the top of the tree.

I wasn't sure how I knew this, I just did.

I also recognized the wooden beads, faded and worn from the years that had been draped around the tree. Jackson and I had been pulled into helping with the tree on more than one occasion.

It had been one of their family activities. One that Mrs. Flynn had implemented every first Sunday after Thanksgiving.

Even though I saw some similarities, the tree had lots of

ornaments on it I didn't recognize. On closer inspection, I saw that they were ornaments from other parts of the country. A ball with the iconic state of Texas on it. Another in the shape of South Carolina with a red and blue light house. A flat ornament from Kansas with a covered wagon painted on it.

Interesting.

The Flynns were doing an impressive job of making the inn a Christmas destination.

I still had the invitation in my pocket that Bianca had handed me. I hadn't even looked at it.

On the second floor, the candles, burned down to stubs, had been blown out. Every night someone, probably still Arabella, came up and blew them all out. They didn't like to leave candles with open flames burning at night.

The fire in the fireplace would be banked, too, after the guests went up to bed, and in the morning they would start the whole process over again.

It seemed like a lot of work, but really it wasn't any more work than going down a checklist before taking an airplane in the air. The same checklist every time. Another checklist after landing.

Letting myself in my room, I went to the window and gazed out at the full moon.

Being back here brought back a lot of memories.

It was different from going home to where my parents lived in Arizona. Home might be where your family was, but there was something to be said for that family living in the same place.

Maybe it was because I thought of the Flynns as my second family.

And by default, that made Alpine Falls, especially the Flynn Manor and the Alpine Lodge a sort of home to me.

Bianca being here had a whole lot to do with my feelings toward being here.

I was getting about as close to having a do-over as a man could get.

And this time I was going to do it right.

I was going to take this second chance at getting to know Bianca and run with it.

If ever there was a time to do it, it was now.

Sixteen

Bianca

When I made my way downstairs to the kitchen and coffee the next morning, Arabella was already up.

She had a bagel in her left hand while manipulating a computer mouse with her right.

I couldn't say a word to her about working too much because I did the very same thing when I was at home.

In fact, I was feeling a little guilty that I had fallen asleep last night without so much as cracking a textbook.

But yesterday had been an unusual day and I gave myself a break about it.

"Good morning," I said.

"Good morning." Arabella glanced up briefly.

"Where is James?" I asked as I popped a pod into the fancy coffee maker.

"He had to go to Houston. An overnighter," she said. "He'll be back later today."

"Huh." I waited for the coffee to heat. "Did Mom and Dad spend the night in Denver?"

"Yeah. It got too late for them to fly back. They might be back today or maybe tomorrow." She closed her computer and looked at me. "How are you?"

"Me? I'm good."

Arabella nodded. "You look rested."

I shoved at my still damp hair. "Really?"

"Did you not sleep well?"

I stirred my coffee. "I slept great."

And I had dreamed about Scott. Not Bradley. Scott.

"Are you about to head over to the lodge?" I asked, changing the subject away from me.

Arabella was looking at me with that intense way she had sometimes. Like she could see right down to my innermost thoughts.

"Soon." She got up. Made herself a second cup of coffee.

"Do you need help with anything?" I asked, cringing at my own words. I had no doubt she would find me something to do. I knew better than to offer.

She added some sweetener to the coffee and stirred it in. Turned back to peer at me over the rim of her coffee cup.

"You don't have anything you need to be doing?"

"Like you," I said with a little shrug. "My work never ends."

"Come on over to the lodge after you finish drying your hair. I'm sure something will come up, but bring some work so I won't feel pressured."

"Haha. Like you ever feel pressured to put people to work."

"So true," she said with a little smirk. "I'm a born leader. That's what James tells me anyway."

"He knows you well."

"I'm just gonna grab a glass of water and head back up." Setting my coffee aside, I filled a glass with water.

"How's Scott Brooks?" Arabella asked after I filled my glass.

"He seems well," I said, hoping she didn't see the way my heart tripped up a notch at the mention of Scott's name. I'd wondered if she had even noticed he was here.

"It's been a long time," she said.

"Ten years," I said, then quickly added. "or so."

"Jackson will be pleased to see him, I'm sure."

"I'm sure he will." I waited a beat. Then went with it. "Do you know if they stayed in touch?"

I picked up my coffee and used it to steady my hands, hiding my expression behind it.

"I don't think so. I haven't heard Jackson say anything about him."

"So he hasn't been back here? Since he left for college?"

"Not that I'm aware of."

Arabella would know. She would definitely know if Scott had stayed in the lodge.

"And yet you recognized him right away," I said.

"Didn't you?"

"Of course. He was practically part of the family when we were growing up."

"I'll give you some time to think about that," Arabella said. "See you at the lodge."

Like I was able to think about much of anything else.

Suddenly ready to get back over to the lodge, I hurried upstairs to finish drying my hair.

While I was at it, I added some loose curls and took the time to put on some mascara.

It was always good for a girl to look her best.

Especially when she just might run into a handsome pilot.

Seventeen

Scott

I got up early the next morning and went into Alpine Falls for breakfast at the little café on Main Street.

The lodge had a perfectly good breakfast menu, but I didn't want to risk running into any of the Flynns this morning. I wanted to have a clear head when I got to my grandfather's house.

I needed to focus on what was best for my mother and Grandpa without the bias of Bianca or her family influencing me.

Since I'd fallen asleep thinking about Bianca and how much I'd like to kiss her again, I knew that I would be easily biased.

Main Street Alpine Falls was just as I remembered it.

Everything that didn't move and a few things that did were draped with colorful twinkling Christmas lights and tinsel and red bows.

Traditional Christmas music spilled from speakers along the sidewalk, but the café played more modern Christmas songs.

I ordered a full breakfast. Eggs. Bacon. Toast.

The server, a young rather flirty high school student smiled and twirled her hair as she took my order.

I didn't complain when she brought my plate with extra bacon and a side of roasted potatoes.

The coffee wasn't up to my standards even after I doused it with sugar and milk.

My next stop would be the coffee shop across the street where I could get a cappuccino.

Like everything in town, it was on the way to Grandpa's house.

While I ate, the train from Denver pulled into the depot and a dozen people got off.

City people.

I smiled at myself for thinking that.

I was a city person myself.

And yet, with my roots here in Alpine Falls, I could spot a city person coming into town from a mile away.

After collecting their luggage, they lined up to wait for the shuttle. I knew the train depot was here, but the shuttle was new. I remembered when people had to walk from the train depot to the lodge, dragging their luggage along behind them.

It was a good thing, having the shuttle, for the town and the lodge.

When I stepped back outside, the music from inside the café blended with the music from the sidewalk into what sounded like an orchestra's warm up session.

I liked it. The festive music. People walking up and down the sidewalks carrying shiny shopping bags.

Most of them were guests of the lodge—there was no hotel in town—but some of the shoppers looked like locals.

I should probably recognize some of them, but I didn't and I doubted they recognized me.

The only reason I recognized the Flynns was because they were like family. And then there was Bianca. That was another story in and of itself.

Cappuccino in hand, I reached Grandpa's house twenty minutes later. A ten minute walk from the café.

The house I'd grown up in, the one that my parents had sold, was two doors down.

I'd walked past my grandparents' house every morning on the way to school and every afternoon on the way home. Passed it every time I walked to the Flynn manor and home again.

I had fond memories of my grandmother having freshly baked cookies on the weekend and my grandfather playing catch with me in the front yard.

I was not prepared to see the house the way it was now.

Shutters were falling off, hanging crooked on either side

of the windows. One of the windows on the second floor was busted out.

The white paint had peeled off showing the dark gray paint beneath it that was from another era.

The lawn where my grandfather had taught me to play catch was grown up with weeds and it looked like someone had used it as a dumping area. Probably kids leaving coke cans and candy wrappers behind after trespassing.

It was a universal fact that kids could not resist an abandoned house.

If I'd thought I was going to be staying here, I had been sorely mistaken. If I'd thought I would simply put it on the market and forget it, I had been wrong.

I took a couple of photos, but didn't have the heart to send them to my mother.

Opening the little wooden gate, squeaking as I pushed it open, I stepped through and braced myself for what I would find on the inside of the house.

Turns out I had not been prepared for that either.

Eighteen

Bianca

I managed all of one hour sitting in front of the fireplace, yellow highlighter in hand, reading through a few pages of my personality psychology textbook.

Just as I had remembered, the warmth of the flames was cozy and relaxing.

It might have been coincidental or maybe I positioned myself so I could see the stairs leading up to the second floor on purpose.

Giving my eyes a break every few minutes, as good an excuse as any, I glanced in that direction.

Maybe I watched for Scott.

To say that Arabella was a master at putting people to work was an understatement.

Tabitha, our sister-in-law, who ran the gift shop on the first floor of the lodge called in sick.

"Will you watch the gift shop this morning?" Arabella asked, perched on the edge of the stone hearth, iPad held against her chest.

"Of course," I said. "Has anything changed?"

"Everything has changed," Arabella said. "Everything is computerized now. But if you can run the cash register, you'll be fine."

"Are you going to show me how to use these new cash registers?" I asked.

"Come on," Arabella said.

The only retail experience I had came from right here in the lodge gift shop. As a family run business, all the Flynn children learned all aspects of the lodge business from the bottom up or inside out as our mother liked to put it.

Fortunately I was a quick study and it didn't take long for Arabella to bring me up to speed on the new system. It helped that it was pretty much scan and click.

At ten o'clock, I turned the sign on the door to "open" and five minutes later I had my first customer. An older gentleman wearing a hat.

"Good morning," I said.

"Good morning. Tabitha isn't here this morning?" he asked, looking past me.

"No. I'm sorry. She was feeling a bit under the weather."

"Oh. I'm so sorry to hear that. I was hoping to get her opinion on a gift for my granddaughter."

"Maybe I can help," I said. "What does she like?"

"The usual college girl things. Maybe I'll just come back later and bring my wife."

"Sure. But I know a bit about college girls if that helps."

"You're in college yourself?"

"Actually I'm a college professor."

The gentleman scrubbed his chin and looked at me, obviously confused.

"I'm just helping out my sister. And Tabitha is my sister-in-law."

"You don't say." He smiled. "I'd heard this was a family run lodge. I guess you and Tabitha are part of that family."

"Don't tell anyone I gave it away," I said in a feigned whisper.

The man laughed. "Don't worry. Your secret is safe with me. Now tell me what college girls like these days."

He left with an Alpine Lodge wool cap, an Alpine Lodge sweatshirt, and a snow globe with a little replica of the lodge inside. I had a feeling his granddaughter was going to be more than pleased.

I stayed steadily busy the rest of the morning. I hadn't remembered the gift shop being this busy, but I'd never worked it at Christmas either.

Tabitha came in at one fifteen, her face flushed.

"I am so sorry," she said. "You don't know how much I appreciate you filling in for me."

"It was kind of fun," I said. "But what about you? Are you feeling better?"

"I'll be okay," she said.

"You're smiling," I said. "What's up with you?"

"It's Christmas," Tabitha said. "What's not to smile about?"

She was right. It was Christmas.

As such I didn't press her. I did, however, file my suspiciousness away for another time.

In the meantime, since I had skipped breakfast, I went in search of lunch. The clean mountain air was good for the appetite.

The lunch crowd had already come and gone at the lounge, so I took a booth and ordered a BLT.

I had no messages from Bradley and I hadn't seen Scott come downstairs today.

It seemed my dilemma with the two men had resolved itself leaving me with no one.

The server brought my food and chatted for a few minutes before going back to work. She'd worked here forever and I asked about her two sons. Both married now. She opened up her phone and showed me photos of her grandbabies.

My gaze was drawn back to the lobby in a quick scan for any sign of Scott.

I found it interesting that I was more concerned that I hadn't seen Scott this morning than I was that I hadn't heard from my boyfriend since yesterday morning.

Maybe there was something wrong with me.

I sent Bradley a text.

> I haven't heard from you. Are you okay?

There. I'd done my part in showing concern.

I stared at the phone. Saw that the message was delivered. But no return message came in, so I set my phone aside.

Obviously I needed to give some serious thought to what was going on with my relationship with Bradley.

Halfway through my lunch, I heard male laughter.

Familiar male laughter.

My brother, Jackson, and Scott sit down at a booth on the other side of the lounge.

They don't see me.

Too nervous to eat now, I push my plate aside. Then dart back to the restroom to wash my hands and rinse my mouth.

While I'm there, I smear on some lip gloss.

Heading back out, I find that my table had been cleared. They'd wasted no time getting it ready for the next person.

Taking the hint, I walked toward the door leading out toward the lobby.

I was only halfway there when Scott looks up and captures my gaze.

His lips turned up into a little smile and I smiled back.

My feet slowed of their own accord and I nearly missed a step.

Standing up, Scott motioned me over.

My brother looked over his shoulder and saw me.

He said something I couldn't quite pick up beneath the joyful Christmas music drifting from the invisible speakers.

Scott was still standing. Waiting for me.

I had no choice but to walk over to their booth.

Nineteen

Scott

I'd no more than gotten back to the stone pathway leading up to the lodge when I ran into Jackson Flynn.

We clapped each other on the back and just like that we picked up where we left off.

"What in the world are you doing here?" he asked. "I wondered who was here in a Skye Travels airplane. Never thought it would be you."

"My mother sent me here to figure out what to do with Grandpa's house."

"I heard he moved to Arizona to live with your parents."

One of the valets opened the door to the lodge and we stepped inside out of the cold.

"Feels nice and warm in here," I said.

"Gotten soft living down in Houston, huh?"

"You wouldn't say that after you survived a summer of Houston heat."

Jackson laughed. "So true. I couldn't do it. You want to get some lunch?"

"Sure."

We walked past the fireplace in the middle of the room, a couple of guests sitting in the oversized chairs, talking. I was pleased to see that they had shiny red Alpine Lodge shopping bags. That was a good sign the business was doing well.

I might not have any investment in the lodge, but it was important to me that it do well.

"So how is Grandpa's house?" Jackson asked. "I haven't been by there."

"I'm not sure it could be much worse." I opened up my phone and showed him the pictures I had taken. "I thought the outside was bad until I saw the inside."

"Didn't know it was that bad," Jackson said. "I could have done something."

"My mother's going to be asking for pictures and I don't have the heart to send her these."

"What are you going to do?" Scott asked as we neared the lounge.

The quietness of the lodge's lobby transitioned into the noisier sounds coming from the lounge. Christmas music. Guests chattering. Silverware clinking.

"I'm gonna go back over there in the morning. Do what I can to clean it up some. Take some more pictures. Then figure what to suggest to my mother. I'm not going to just give it away because it needs some work. It's in a prime location."

"I don't have anything scheduled tomorrow," Jackson said. "You want some help?"

"I wouldn't turn it down," I said as we settled into a booth.

"What time do you want to get started?"

"Have to be there at eight for a delivery of supplies from the General Store."

"Just tell me what time you want me there," Jackson said.

"I'll probably head over about seven. Anytime that's—" I stopped in mid-sentence, forgetting what I'd been going to say.

Bianca walked toward us.

She looked different. More relaxed. Her hair curled softly over her shoulders and her eyes were bright. Her lips shiny.

I stood up.

Jackson looked over his shoulder, following my gaze.

"There's Bianca. We should get her to help."

"She can't do that kind of work," I said, motioning her over.

I'd been thinking about her all day and here she was.

"I don't see why not," Jackson said.

I didn't tell Jackson that his sister wasn't built for manual labor and that was something I would never ask her to do.

"Hi," I said as Bianca reached the booth.

"Hi." She glanced at Jackson. "Hey Jack."

"Hey Sis."

"Do you have time to sit?" I asked, moving aside for her to sit with us.

She shrugged. "For a minute."

I didn't miss the look Jackson gave us as Bianca slid into the booth and I sat next to her.

Somewhere along the way the past and present had folded up on each other, for me at least, and Jackson had quite a bit of catching up to do.

Twenty

Bianca

Lunch time turned into afternoon and the lounge had cleared out for the most part.

I watched as my brother and Scott ate hamburgers and talked about how they would go about making his grandfather's house presentable, supposedly in one day.

Somehow Scott had mesmerized me into sliding into the booth next to him.

That had to be what happened.

It had to be that he'd mesmerized me.

What other explanation could there be for the way I couldn't stop looking at him? For the way I smiled every time he glanced in my direction?

I jumped when my phone chimed with a text.

A quick glance told me it was Bradley. Finally.

As the men kept talking I read the text.

BRADLEY

I don't think I'm going to make it up there. They need someone to be on call Christmas. I drew the short straw.

There was no drawing of the straws. I knew Bradley well enough to know that there didn't need to be. He loved his job.

If there was a need for someone to be on call, he would volunteer.

Besides, his family lived right there in Denver, so he could spend Christmas with his family while darting in to work if needed.

"Everything okay?" Scott asked.

"It's just a work thing." I waved it off and set my phone back down, face down, without responding.

It was a work thing. Just not my work thing.

"Do you need to go?" Jackson asked.

"I'm okay."

"You gonna come help us tomorrow?" Jackson asked.

"She can't do that kind of work," Scott said. "She's a professional."

Jackson looked at me sideways.

My brother, obviously, didn't see me the same way Scott did.

Scott was being very protective.

"She can be moral support then," Jackson said. "And bring us food."

"That's a little sexist," I said, feigning offense. I actually didn't mind. I was rather enjoying having Scott in this unexpected protective role.

Maybe I taught the importance of gender equality in my psychology classes, but the truth was evolution was evolution. There was a reason men were bigger and stronger than women.

And there was a reason women were attracted to men who could take care of them whether financially or physically. I would not apologize for liking those differences, nor would I be offended when they were pointed out. Not by Scott. My brother. Maybe.

"I would be okay with that," Scott said. "But not in a sexist way. We're gonna need someone there to keep us in line. Besides. I wouldn't mind the company."

Jackson looked from one of us to the other and back again.

"Did I miss something?" he asked.

"No," Scott and I both said at the same time.

It was a lie and all three of us sitting there at the table knew it.

I just didn't know what that something was and I was pretty sure I wasn't alone in that. All I knew was that Scott had blindsided me and then he'd mesmerized me.

"I've got to run down to the airfield," Jackson said, looking at his phone. "Christopher is back with our parents and they need help getting everything to the house."

He looked at us.

"I guess I'll see you in the morning," he said to Scott.

"See you."

"We have managed to completely baffle my brother," I said.

Scott smiled. "He's easily confused. Always has been."

"I guess so." I watched my brother walk across the lounge toward the doors. "You have to admit, though, he has a good reason in this case."

Scott put his arm on the back of the booth in a classic male move.

I took a deep breath. Let it out slowly.

"There's something I need to tell you," I said.

Twenty-One

Scott

There's something I need to tell you was right up there with *we need to talk*.

Two phrases a guy never wanted to hear from the girl he was interested in.

"You've got a boyfriend," I said.

Even though I said it with an air of nonchalance, I wasn't feeling nonchalant. I was feeling, instead, rather deflated.

When Bianca's eyes widened, the feeling settled in and I shifted my perspective to accept it.

"How did you know?" she asked.

"Because a girl like you always has a boyfriend. And I knew by the way you said it."

"A girl like me? What does that mean?"

"Professional. Kind." I was not a faint of heart kind of guy, so I went with the truth. "Beautiful."

I looked into her eyes as I said the words. Her emerald green eyes had always fascinated me. She was like a siren and I was a hapless sailor being beckoned onto the rocks.

She looked away.

"I sort of have a boyfriend. Maybe."

"Sort of and maybe."

"He was supposed to come home with me, but he... He has to work."

"He chose work." I knew the kind.

"Yes," she said. "He chose work."

The kind of guy a girl like Bianca should put in the rearview mirror.

"He sounds like an idiot," I said.

That brought a smile back to her lips.

"He might be."

"Not might be. Definitely is."

"At any rate, he isn't coming." She frowned. "Jackson didn't know he was coming though."

"Jackson's confusion comes from a whole different angle."

"I suppose it does."

"Do you want to get out of here? Take a walk downtown?"

"Didn't you just come from downtown?"

"That was different. That was work. Unless you already have plans."

"Nothing more than a standing appointment with a textbook."

"How about I buy you an ice cream cone?"

"You do know the way to a girl's heart."

I grinned. "Just give me a chance, Beautiful."

Not waiting for a response, I stood up and held out a hand to help her slide out of the booth.

"I need to run up to my room for a minute," I said. "Meet you at the front doors in ten?"

"Okay. I'll get my coat."

I strode across the lobby and dashed up the stairs.

Reaching the second story, I turned right and started down the long hallway.

The candles behind the glass globes, flickered as I walked past.

"I know that's not possible," I said and kept walking.

A trick of the light. That's all it was.

A trick of the light that people mistook for something otherworldly.

As a pilot, I knew all about illusions and such. False horizons. Runway width illusions. Autokinesis.

I wasn't falling for this one.

Just as I reached my door, my phone rang.

I checked the caller id.

It was my mother.

I hated to do it, but I was going to have to stretch the truth.

Otherwise, she'd have me sending pictures she most certainly did not want to see.

I'd just tell her the truth.

I'd gotten distracted.

Twenty-Two

Bianca

I grabbed my coat from the cloak room near the kitchen, and made my way toward the front door to wait for Scott.

"Hey," Arabella said, holding up a hand as I passed by the front desk.

"Hey." I kept walking.

"Do you have time…?"

"Sorry," I said. "I've got plans." Whatever it was, she would have to get someone else to help her. I really did have other plans.

I didn't see her smile to herself as I kept walking.

Pulling my phone out of my pocket, I reread Bradley's text message.

They were just typed words on the screen, but I heard the satisfaction in them. Bradley was still young enough that he took it as an honor to be asked to work more. It made him feel important.

Work was his thing. His life.

For a little while, I'd thought I might be his thing. His life. Or at least a close second.

But it didn't surprise me that he had chosen work. Flat out chosen work.

I wasn't surprised. And I wasn't upset about it.

Part of that could be Scott walking down the stairs, seeing me, and smiling.

Maybe more than just a little part.

I sent Bradley a quick response.

> Thanks for the update. Merry Christmas.

I hit send.

And with sending that message, I put Bradley out of my head.

"Ready?" Scott asked.

"Ready."

I waved at Tabitha as I passed by the gift shop. She still looked happier than I had ever seen her and that was saying something.

The valet opened the door and we stepped outside into the bitingly cold wind.

"It's going to snow," I said with a glance up toward the

tall mountains, their peaks hidden behind layers of white clouds banked around them.

"Won't be long," Scott agreed.

"You don't have snow in Houston, do you?" I asked. "Or Arizona."

"Not really. Rarely."

We started down the stone pathway leading to the main road. Random blue spruce trees were scattered about. Pine trees. Maple trees. The blue spruce trees were the only ones that still had leaves.

"Do you miss it?"

"I miss a lot of things," he said, glancing over at me with a little smile. "What about you? Do you miss Alpine Falls?"

"Sometimes I do. There are things I miss."

I reached out and ran my fingers along the rough needles of a blue spruce tree.

I missed the way the spruce trees smelled after a rain or when they were covered with a layer of snow.

I missed the way we could walk to town in fifteen minutes. The way the town was decorated for Christmas. Colorful twinkling lights. Red bows.

Music spilling from hidden speakers.

An old pickup truck rumbled passed, the trunk loaded up with chopped firewood.

A family walked past us on their way back to the lodge.

There were so many little things that I missed whenever I allowed myself to think about it.

And now I was going to miss Scott.

Twenty-Three

Scott

"Do you still like pistachio and mint chocolate chip?" I asked as we stood in line at the ice cream shop.

"How do you remember that?" Bianca asked, looking at me sideways.

"I remember it because it was a little strange. And." I lowered my head to whisper in her ear. "Jackson used to make fun of you."

She rolled her eyes. "Jackson made fun of everything."

"A sign of a good brother," I said, coming to the defense of my friend.

"Pals before gals?" she asked with obvious amusement.

"Something like that," I said. "And that's why a guy shouldn't date his brother's sister."

"I knew you would come up with a reason," she said. We were next up to the counter. "Do you still like plain vanilla?"

"I do not," I said with indignation. "I get one scoop of vanilla and one scoop of chocolate." It pleased me inordinately that she remembered that I preferred plain vanilla ice cream.

She smiled. "You've changed so much."

"I didn't think you noticed what I liked," I said.

"How could I not? It was just so... plain. I felt bad for you."

"Bad for me? Why would you feel bad for me?"

"Because you didn't know what you were missing."

"I know now," I said just before we stepped up to the counter to place our order.

I ordered for her. What could I say? I was a little old fashioned. And we were in a place that lent itself to a guy being old fashioned. If a guy couldn't be old fashioned in Alpine Falls, then where could he be old fashioned?

We took a seat at a little table for two near the window to wait for our ice cream.

The table tops were a cheerful red. Just as I remembered. They had to have been refinished recently. They were too perfect and unscuffed.

A little Christmas tree stood behind us, decorated all in birds. That was different.

Bianca looked over her shoulder to see what I was looking at.

"Birds," she said. "Reminds me of my grandmother."

"Birds remind you of your grandmother?"

"No. The birds on the tree remind me of my grandmother, my mother's mother. She lived a simple life."

"You say that like you envy her," I said turning my attention from the tree back to Bianca.

"I don't have anything to be envious of. My life wasn't complicated. Just busy."

"What about now?" I asked. "Is it complicated now?"

"Not so much," she said with a little smile.

"What about the boyfriend?"

"I don't think he's a boyfriend so much anymore."

"So much?" I couldn't help but wonder if it was wrong that I felt a burst of happiness that her relationship with her boyfriend was over.

"Well," she said. "It seems like I should tell him before I declare it over."

"You could text him," I said.

"Maybe later."

"Here," I said, holding out a hand. "I can text him for you."

She laughed a little nervously. "You can't do that."

"I'm not scared. I'll do it."

"Why?" she asked. "Why do you want to text him?"

I pulled my hand back and looked into her emerald green eyes.

"Once you tell him," I said. "I can kiss you again."

Confusion crossed her face along with a pretty blush of color.

"I think you already did that," she said.

"But I didn't know," I said. "So it didn't count against me."

She swallowed. "It counted," she said, so softly I could barely hear her.

"Didn't say it didn't count," I said just as softly. "I just said it didn't count against me."

I was falling so hard and fast, it was making my head spin.

My only consolation was that I didn't have far to fall.

Twenty-Four

Bianca

I scooped up a bite of pistachio ice cream. Added a touch of the green mint.

And closed my eyes as I savored it.

When I opened my eyes, Scott was watching me.

"They have the best ice cream here," I said.

"Surely they have good ice cream in Denver," Scott said.

"Maybe. I haven't looked."

"Your boyfriend doesn't take you out for ice cream?"

"He's not my boyfriend anymore."

"Officially."

With every passing minute I spent with Scott, I was

feeling more and more like Bradley was already in my history.

Somehow I had circled back around and picked up my childhood crush. Someone I hadn't expected to even see again.

It was like Scott and Bradley had exchanged seats. So easily and naturally. All in one day.

As I took a bite of mint chocolate chip ice cream, I wondered if I should be concerned about that.

I didn't play games with men. In fact, I rarely dated.

I'd dated Bradley as long as I'd dated anyone.

And yet I'd just tossed him aside like a carton of expired milk.

Not officially though. I had to tell him first.

It was a rule I had come up with in the heat of the moment, but I was sticking to it.

Rules were the glue that held civilization together, after all.

I told myself it was Bradley's fault for blowing me off so easily for work.

But I knew it was more than that.

I knew it was Scott.

If Scott hadn't been sitting here teasing me about my choice of ice cream and making me realize that Bradley hadn't taken me out for ice cream, not even once, I wouldn't be thinking about how to officially break it off with Bradley.

Somehow, despite what I'd said, it didn't seem right to break up with Bradley via text.

But since I was here and he was in Denver and I was

thinking about kissing Scott, then maybe it was better than not telling him anything at all.

Maybe it was better than just letting him believe that everything was the same as it had been the last time I'd seen him.

What was it? Almost two weeks ago?

Maybe he and I didn't go out all that often.

But we had made plans to come to Alpine Falls together.

He had just brushed me off.

And now Scott was looking at me with his mesmerizing blue eyes. The way he was looking at me had me almost believing that he hadn't dated at all whatsoever over the last ten years.

That he had just been waiting for me to come back into his life.

I knew an easy enough way to dispel that thought.

"You're not seeing anyone?" I asked.

"No," he said.

"So you have lots of different girlfriends?"

He almost looked hurt.

"Why would you say that?" he asked.

"My brothers talk about how pilots have a girl in every port."

"Some do," he said. "But I don't."

"Why not?" I asked.

He looked so serious now.

"It's not my style." He stacked our empty ice cream cups together and got up to drop them in the trash.

I felt like I had stepped on a sore spot.

But it made no sense. We were just talking about dating.

"Do you want to walk around?" he asked, changing the subject as he sat back down next to me.

"Sure." Whatever it was, he didn't want to talk about it. so I had to let it go.

He had me curious now, though.

Curious about how a red-blooded American airplane pilot didn't want to talk about dating.

There was only one explanation I could come up with.

Someone had hurt him.

Twenty-Five

Scott

Christmas music spilled all around us as Bianca and I walked down Main Street and stepped into a little gift shop.

It was different from the gift shop at the lodge.

Unlike the lodge, this gift shop had a million different items.

They had rows of Colorado and Alpine Falls coffee mugs. As many t-shirts.

And they had displays of post cards, necklaces in the shape of colorful aspen leaves, and a section just for chocolate fudge in all different flavors.

Although most people would call it a souvenir store, it was what my mother would affectionately call a "junk store."

We walked up and down the aisles, not looking at anything in particular.

I picked up a baseball cap. Set it on her head.

"Now that's a cute look," I said.

"Right. A baseball cap over a wool cap."

"I have a good imagination," I said. "In Houston you wouldn't need the wool cap."

"I would think not. I don't think I could survive the heat."

"You don't really have to. We have covered parking and everything is air conditioned."

"Still. You have to get to your car."

"True. That can be tricky sometimes."

I didn't tell her that I had a car I could start remotely so my car would be cool when I got inside.

Despite being able to imagine what she would look like in a baseball cap—no wool cap—I was having a hard time imagining her in Houston.

She was a mountain girl. Not a south Texas girl.

I'd never even seen her wearing shorts.

That's something I would have remembered.

"Do you have any Christmas gifts to buy?" I asked her.

"Here? No. I bought them all in Denver."

We walked past a display of candles in the shape of birds. What was with the birds in Alpine Falls anyway?

"What about you?" she asked. "Do you have gifts to buy?"

"Maybe," I said.

"Do you think your family would enjoy a gift from Alpine Falls?"

"I don't know. Maybe. I'll get them gift cards."

Bianca stopped and lifted her chin to look up at me. It was a startling reminder that she was a full head shorter than I was. Perfect height for me.

"You can't give them gift cards."

"Why not?"

She started walking again. "It's too impersonal."

"Okay," I said. "What do you suggest?"

She seemed to consider as she scanned the store.

"Candles for your sister and your mother," she said. "Coffee mugs for your father and grandfather. Then you can give them gift cards, too."

"Okay," I said.

This was a new experience for me.

A girl who knew my entire family without me telling her about them.

Since I'd never brought a girl home, to here or Arizona, everyone else started out at a disadvantage.

I picked up a candle, popped off the lid, and sniffed. It smelled like green apples. I held it over for Bianca to sniff.

"That's nice," she said, then picked up another one. Sniffed it. "This one, too."

She held it over for me. It smelled like Christmas cookies.

"My mother will definitely like this one," I said.

"Now we just need a couple of mugs."

"Three," I said.

"Three?" She picked up a big Alpine Falls mug. Turned it this way and that. "Why three?"

"We have to get one for my sister's husband."

"No way. Marianne got married?"

"About five years ago."

"Who to?" She replaced the mug on the shelf.

"You wouldn't know him. Some guy she met at college."

"Is he nice? Do you like him?"

"He treats my sister well, so yeah. I like him."

"Good," she said, picking up another mug. "It's weird when our siblings get married, isn't it? Having new people with us on Christmas mornings."

"It is rather odd. But it's okay. You should be used to having a lot of people over at your house."

"I am." She shrugged and picked out two mugs. "These are nice. Get these. It's different though, right? When they're married?"

"How so?" I followed her toward the checkout counter.

"Sometimes they go to visit their families. It just makes everything... I don't know. Imperfect."

After I paid and the checker wrapped everything up, put it in one of the bright shiny shopping bags, we headed out.

"I wouldn't do that," I said, holding the door open for her to walk through.

"You wouldn't do what?"

"I wouldn't go off and visit my own family on Christmas."

"Yes, you would," she said. "You would have to. They're your family."

"Right," I said. But I knew that I was right.

I'd spent more time at the Flynn's house on Christmas as a teenager than with my own family.

And even though I'd bought gifts for my sister and her husband, at Bianca's insistence, I didn't even know if they were going to Arizona for Christmas or if they were going to spend Christmas with her husband and his family in Pennsylvania. Last I heard they hadn't decided.

Didn't matter. I'd enjoyed shopping with Bianca.

Now I just needed to get her something.

What did a guy get for a girl like Bianca? It couldn't be anything from the lodge or even Alpine Falls. It had to be something special.

Twenty-Six

Bianca

I tightened my scarf as I walked next to Scott downtown Alpine Falls.

The Christmas music was joyful and my heart swelled with the magic of it all.

I'd always liked Christmas, but this was turning out to be different and special.

I thought about what he'd said. He'd said he wouldn't spend Christmas with his family.

Why would he tell me that?

And what did he mean by it?

Thinking back to ten years ago, all my teenage Christmas memories included Scott. Scott as my brother's best friend.

He had gone home some. I was certain of it. Even though I couldn't remember him actually leaving.

"Ready to head back?" he asked.

"Sure. You have to be up early in the morning."

He glanced up toward the jagged mountain peaks.

"I have a feeling it's going to be cold in the morning."

"Did you check the forecast?" I asked.

He looked at me sideways. "I did not."

She smiled. "Let me guess. You don't have to look."

"You must hear that a lot."

"I do hear it a lot. And I'm the same way, truth be known."

"However," I said. "I will check it before I fly out."

I bit my lip.

I didn't ask when he was flying out. I wanted to ask, but at the same time, I didn't want to know.

I wanted him to stay right here.

To spend Christmas with us just like he did back when we lived here.

We passed the little tree lined park. The park had a little walkway that led down to the river. Benches. And a little bubbling fountain.

I never went that way simply because I walked beside the river on my family property every time I walked to the lodge and back.

This park, as far as I was concerned, was for tourists.

But Scott turned that way.

"The old fountain is still here," he said.

"Everything is still here."

But we walked up and stood in front of it.

It was a simple fountain. Water bubbling up out of rocks and cascading down. Rocks taken from somewhere, maybe from the river.

"We have to make a wish," he said.

"A wish?" I looked over at him. He was smiling as he reached into his pocket and pulled out two coins. "You still carry coins?"

"Only for wishes," he said, pressing one into my gloved hand.

"What do we wish for?" I asked.

"Something that would make you happy," he said.

I looked at the coin in my hand. A quarter.

A Christmas wish.

Turns out that was easy.

Twenty-Seven

Scott

Sometimes I just made things up as I went.

Like the wish at the fountain.

Maybe I'd heard about doing it at some point, but I'd never actually made a wish at the fountain.

But then I'd never walked near the park with a girl either.

It would have been weird if Jackson and I had made wishes at the fountain. That would never happen.

In fact, we'd put soap in the fountain once. Now that had been fun.

Unfortunately the adults in town hadn't liked it very much.

Bianca tossed the quarter from one mittened hand to the other. She looked to be in serious thought.

"You don't have any wishes?" I asked.

She glanced over at me. "I have lots of wishes."

"I see. So it's hard to pick one."

"Maybe," she said.

Then she closed her eyes and tossed the coin into the fountain.

"What did you wish for?" I asked.

"I can't tell you that."

"It was worth a try," I said impishly.

She rolled her eyes.

"Your turn," she said.

I tossed my quarter into the fountain.

"Mine was easy."

"Yeah? What did you wish for?" she asked.

"Christmas snow," I said.

"Liar," she said.

"Can't a guy wish for snow?"

"It's going to snow anyway, so it would be a wasted wish and you know it."

"I guess you'll never know then."

"If it comes true, you can tell me," she said.

"Where did that rule come from?"

"I made it up. I'm a professor. I can do that."

I laughed. "I'm beginning to get a more clear picture."

"You're bad." She bumped me with her elbow.

"Me? You're the one making up rules as you go. First the breaking up thing. And now the wish thing."

"You're keeping up rather well," she said.

"Don't ever underestimate my powers of keeping up."

"I don't underestimate anything."

We continued our walk back toward the lodge.

Somehow time had passed and the sun had dropped over the mountain peaks, leaving us in the faded sunlight of early evening.

As we neared the lodge it became more and more evident to me that I wasn't ready to let Bianca go.

"Have dinner with me," I said.

"Okay." She didn't even hesitate.

That in itself gave me hope that my Christmas wish just might have some chance of coming true.

Twenty-Eight

Bianca

Scott and I walked back to the lodge in the faded sunlight of early evening.

I'd spent the last few minutes trying to think of some excuse to keep him around. I even wondered if Arabella might have some task that we needed to do. A task that did not involve going into the attic, but a task that Scott and I could do together.

"Have dinner with me," he said.

I agreed without hesitation.

I'd never played games and now was not the time for me to start playing coy.

Dinner, even though, it was a little early and I wasn't

hungry, sounded like as good an excuse to spend more time together as any.

My Christmas wish at the fountain had been easy. I knew what I wanted to wish for, but I'd given it some thought, probably too much, as to how to word it.

It was just a Christmas wish. Something that couples did together. And maybe children. Children and couples.

Scott and I were neither of those things, but I'd known what to wish for nonetheless.

We walked toward the lodge, on the trail leading through the blue spruce trees in easy companionship.

I wondered what Arabella and Jackson would think about me spending time with Scott.

Arabella hadn't seemed to think anything of it. But Jackson. Jackson had looked confused. And that made me smile.

"You're smiling," Scott pointed out as the front doors to the lodge came into view.

"Just thinking," I said.

"You're smiling that secret smile like women do when they know something no one else does."

I stopped right there on the path and looked at him.

"Tabitha," I said.

"What?"

"Tabitha. She came in late today and she was smiling. Like you just said. I think I might know why."

"Why?"

"It's just my theory, so you can't tell anyone."

"Scout's honor."

He hadn't been in the scouts, but I'd take it.

"I think she might be pregnant," I whispered as though the trees had ears.

"Oh. Wow. That's big."

"I could be wrong," I said with a shrug and started walking again. "Probably just what she said. It's Christmas and she's married to my brother. She's happy."

"She said that?"

"She said she was happy because it's Christmas. I made up the part about my brother."

"There you go making stuff up again. I'm gonna have to watch you."

"Probably."

The valet opened the door and we went inside.

"It always feels so good in here," Scott said.

"Houston has ruined you," I said.

"Probably."

We made our way across the lobby. There were people sitting around the oversized fireplace. It would be like this now through Christmas and New Year's.

I didn't mind. It was a good sign that Arabella's attempts to make the lodge a holiday destination were working.

She'd been talking about adding on a New Year's Eve party to her already busy Christmas season activities.

If anyone could do it, Arabella could.

Speaking of Arabella, she wasn't behind the front desk or anywhere in sight.

Maybe she had gone home early for a change.

Stepping into the lounge was like stepping into a

different world. There was music and people talking and servers running back and forth to the kitchen.

The lounge had a charm all its own. Different from the charm of the lodge.

I often wondered how that could be.

Two places in the same building feeling so different.

We took a booth at the far end near the window overlooking the lobby.

This was starting to feel natural.

Twenty-Nine

Scott

Sitting at a booth across from Bianca with the noises of the lounge—Christmas music, conversations—swirling all around us felt right.

More than right.

It felt natural.

I'd sat here in the lounge a hundred times with Jackson, during the day when it was a café. Not at night. As teenagers, we weren't allowed in the lounge at night.

"Did you ever think you would come back here?" Bianca asked. "For any reason?"

"I don't know. I hate to say never. But once my parents

moved to Arizona and Jackson moved to Denver, I couldn't see any reason to."

And Bianca had moved away, too. But that didn't figure into the equation at the time.

It was part of the equation now.

Just one look at her and I knew. All the feelings for her I'd tamped down were right there on the surface.

And apparently feelings were a bit strange. Sometimes they dissolved with time. In my case, my feelings had only gotten stronger.

Or maybe it was just that I was willing to entertain them now unlike back in high school.

Bianca tucked a strand of hair behind an ear and ordered a sparkling water.

Wondering if her hair was as soft as it looked, I ordered the same.

"So," I said. "Have you given any more thought about sending that text message?"

"No," she said with a little laugh. "It seems like the kind of thing that should be done in person, doesn't it?"

"Maybe." I took a sip of my water. "He's in Denver?"

"Yes."

"Want me to fly you down there? Get this thing over with?"

"There might be something wrong with you," she said with a little laugh. Then she sobered. "Wait. You're serious."

"I've done more for less," I said. "But no pressure." I held up a hand. "I understand if you aren't ready to move on."

Scowling at me, she bit her lip. "Let's talk about something else."

"Okay. What?"

"Tell me about Houston."

"It's hot. Awful traffic."

"But you like it."

I tilted my head. "You're a mind reader?"

"I've been accused." She held a straight face as she said it.

"Now you're scaring me a little bit."

She smiled that secret smile again. "Don't worry. I'm licensed to do a little mind reading."

I sat back, sipped my water, and studied her.

"I'm going to let that go for now," I said. "But yes. I do like it."

She nodded slowly. And I would have loved to know what was going on in that pretty head of hers. What was she thinking?

Was she thinking what I was thinking?

Wondering if there the slightest realm of possibility that she and I could continue past tonight?

"What do you like most about it?" she asked.

"The traffic," I said.

"The awful traffic you just told me about?"

"I prefer it over winding mountain roads. Besides, I like the challenge."

"That fits," she said, thoughtfully. "The way you and Jackson went after the video games."

"We did, didn't we?"

"You did."

"The funny thing is that even though I attribute a lot of my flying skills to video games, Noah Worthington prefers that we read books when we have down time."

"I know Noah. He's a smart man."

"I agree."

"So, really? You've taken up reading?"

"Don't look at me like that."

She put the back of her hand over her mouth. "It's just hard for me to picture. Let me guess. Science fiction?"

"Of course." I looked past her, a red shirt catching my attention. "Your sister is heading this way."

"Oh no." Bianca groaned. "I am not going up in the attic."

Thirty

Bianca

"I need you to go back into the attic," Arabella said.

Scott was grinning and not even trying to hide it.

"What could you possibly need from the attic now?" I asked.

"Christmas decorations," Arabella said.

"Don't we have enough?" I swept my hand in a general direction.

The lodge was decorated to the hilt. Not just the huge tree covered in decorations. The garland wrapped around the banisters. The lives pots of poinsettias on every table.

"It's for the tree decorating contest."

"Which you discontinued last year."

"People are asking for it," she said.

I looked over at Scott with skepticism.

He was staying out of this one. He knew how I felt about the attic, especially at night.

Arabella set the key on the table. "It's not until tomorrow night, so just whenever."

Whenever.

After she walked off, presumptuously leaving the key on the table, I looked over at Scott.

"Maybe you and Jackson can go up and get the decorations."

"Wait a minute," Scott said. "Is there something you aren't telling me?"

"No." I shifted in my seat. Picked up a menu I didn't need to look at.

"It sure does seem like it," he said. "I don't have to be a licensed psychologist... or a licensed mind reader... to see just how uncomfortable the attic makes you."

"I've never seen anything," she said, turning her lovely green eyes on me. "But I've made it a point to stay away from the attic."

"Because."

"Because my sister, Arabella, of all people, has. And our parents told her that she... Abigail..." I whispered the name and glanced around as though just saying it might conjure her up. "was her imaginary friend."

"I did not know that."

"I'm pretty sure Jackson has seen her, too."

"What does she look like?"

"I don't know," I said. "And it bothers me that you want to know."

"I'm just curious because maybe I've seen her and didn't know it. I mean does she look like a regular person or does she look like a... you know... specter?"

"I don't know," I said. "I think she looks like a regular person."

I was feeling decidedly uncomfortable.

Ghosts might be real. Might not.

I was willing to live and let... well... live. As long as they didn't bother me, I wouldn't bother them.

If they were real, I did not need to know. Actually I didn't need to know one way or another.

"We should order something," I said. And maybe Jackson or one of the other guys in the family would show up and could go up to the attic with Scott.

It wasn't that I didn't want to spend time with Scott. I did.

But just not in the attic.

"What would you like?" he asked.

"I think I'll have the shrimp sandwich."

"Ah," Scott said. "The seafood is another of my favorite things about Houston. Is it good here?"

"I think so. But I don't have a coastal city to compare it to."

"That's something I can help you with." He rubbed his hands together. "Let's do it."

I'd never known just how much fun Scott could be. I

could most definitely see why he and my brother had been best friends.

I was most definitely going to miss him.

Thirty-One

Scott

I would say that I have some decent powers of persuasion.

Getting Bianca to agree to go into the attic with me had taken all of them.

I didn't push her too hard though.

I'd just told her I would go by myself. Send her pictures and she could tell me what to bring down.

"This is getting to be too much," she said as we walked along the second floor hallway toward the attic door.

"What's getting to be too much?" I asked.

"That," she said with a nod toward the candles flickering as we walked past.

"Are they real?" I asked.

She stopped right there in the middle of the hallway and looked at me.

"Let's be empiricists. Pick up one of the glass globes."

"Okay," I said, walking over to the nearest sconce on the wall. I looked over my shoulder.

"It's okay," she said.

I wasn't exactly sure I wanted to do this. But Bianca made an excellent point.

If they were real candles, they should not be flickering. But they were flickering. There had to be an explanation.

I put a hand on the glass globe, but almost jerked it away. It was icy cold, but it quickly warmed beneath my hand.

"Very strange," I said.

"What?" Bianca stayed back, watching me from several feet away.

"Nothing. I just thought it felt cold for a minute."

I lifted the globe and the candle immediately stopped flickering.

Confused, I grasped the bottom of the candle, avoiding the rivulets of wax on the sides. Lifted it up out its little seat.

Holding the candle, still not flickering, I turned and held it out for Bianca to see.

"It stopped flickering," I said, fascinated. It wasn't wired up to electricity. It wasn't an illusion.

The other candles along the wall had stopped flickering, too.

"What do you make of it?" I asked her.

"I don't know," Bianca said. "I don't want to know."

"It's fascinating," I said, putting it back in its holder and replacing the globe.

I took a step back and waited for it to start flickering again.

It didn't.

I ran a hand through my hair. I suppose I had deep down thought the flickering candles were some kind of illusion or maybe even something electric.

But nope. That was not it.

"Have you seen this before?" I asked Bianca.

She shook her head. "I don't think so."

"It's fascinating."

"It's creepy."

She grabbed my arm and dragged me toward the attic door.

"Let's get this over with," she said.

Even though I went along with her, I wasn't convinced. I wanted to do some more exploring of the candles.

Why had Jackson and I never seen anything like this? We would have figured it out.

Bianca's hands trembled as she went to put the key in the lock.

"Here," I said, putting a hand gently over hers. "Let me help you."

She put the key in my palm.

"You're shaking like a leaf," I said. "Let's go back downstairs. We don't have to do this."

"Let's just get it over with," she said. I could literally see her squaring her shoulders.

"You sure?"

"I'm sure."

"Okay then." I pushed the door open. The musty, earthy, and damp scent of the attic filled my senses.

"How does the attic smell damp?" I asked.

"I always wondered that."

"Want me to go first?" I asked.

"No. I'll go," she said, going through the door and heading up the stairs.

I smiled after her.

Way to face your fears.

I was impressed.

Thirty-Two

Bianca

Kneeling in front of one of the trunks in the section of the attic unofficially designated for Christmas decorations, I shoved open the heavy lid. Scott caught it before it fell back, letting it down slowly.

"What are we looking for?" he asked.

"Anything that's not sentimental that guests can use for decorating trees."

"A decorating contest? Did I hear that right?"

"You did. My sister has all sorts of activities to keep the guests busy at Christmas."

"It's a good thing you're here then," he said. "I wouldn't know what's sentimental."

He picked up a strand of worn wooden beads. "Except this. I saw some of these on the big tree."

"I think you know more than you think you do."

My hands were a little more steady now as I moved the beads aside and looked under them.

The thing with the flickering candles had freaked me out a little. I had no explanation for it and Scott seemed intent on messing with them.

The worst of it was I had told him to do it.

I hadn't expected it to be so drastically obvious that something inexplicable was going on with the candles.

"Everything in here looks sentimental to me," Scott said.

"Agreed. Let's close this one up and go to the next one."

I sat on my heels as he closed the lid and fastened it. The trunk itself must be about a hundred years old.

It was worn with cracked leather that needed to be conditioned. The belt on it was starting to rust.

Someone should really take better care of our family's antiques. I made a mental note to tell Arabella that we should bring some of this stuff downstairs and use it for something. As for what, I didn't know. Arabella was good at the decorating part. It seemed like a waste to leave it up here in the attic.

We went to the next trunk and opened it up.

This was more what we were looking for.

These Christmas decorations were obviously new and some of them still had tags on them. There were glittery balls in blue and some in silver. Rolls of tinsel that might be outdated, but had never been used.

"This is what we're looking for," he said.

"Let's put this one by the door and see if we can find one more to go with it."

Turns out we found three more boxes in addition to the trunk.

I did my job of holding the door while Scott took them down the stairs.

Every time he left me standing at the top of the stairs, I squeezed my eyes closed and repeated what became something of a mantra.

There is nothing to be afraid of. There are no ghosts. There is nothing to be afraid of. There are no ghosts. There is nothing to be afraid of.

I couldn't say that I actually believed it, but it seemed to help.

"This is it," Scott said, picking up the last of the boxes.

"It's more than we thought we'd find." This time I hurried down before him throwing open the door leading out into the hallway.

Two people walked down the hall, deep in conversation. Even though they went into their room, I immediately felt better just knowing that someone else was there. Someone alive and well.

The candles along the wall were not flickering. Just burning straight and steady behind their glass sconces.

Scott stacked the boxes and carrying two of them, we walked in silence, neither of us feeling the need to point out the obvious.

The further we got away from the attic, the more relieved I felt.

"Hey," Jackson said, glancing at me, then Scott as we reached the front desk. "There you are. You need some help?"

"There's a trunk and another box just outside the attic door if you want to grab them," Scott said.

"The attic," Jackson said, his face going blank. "Sure."

I shrugged when he glanced at me.

I knew he would go. He would go because Scott asked him to.

No other reason.

"Well," Jackson said, rubbing his hands on his jeans. "I'll be right back then."

Scott carried the boxes into one of the back rooms and set them down.

"Him too, huh?"

I just shrugged.

Thirty-Three

Scott

What was it with Bianca and Jackson and the attic?

The Jackson I knew would be like me. Ready and eager to go exploring anything that seemed out of the ordinary, especially something that might suggest the possibility of a ghost.

But here he was acting like Bianca. Like he didn't want to go near the attic.

"Do we need to do anything else tonight?" I asked after the boxes were all tucked away for tomorrow's activity.

"I don't think so," Bianca said, glancing at her watch.

"Can I walk you home?"

"Okay. Just don't tell Arabella. She doesn't like us to walk the trails in the dark."

"I won't tell."

We walked through the lobby, past the four-sided fireplace. Guests relaxing in the chairs around it. The Christmas tree standing tall and elegant, lights twinkling like fireflies.

"I'm impressed how busy the lodge is this time of year."

"It's become something of a destination. The train helped. Then the helicopter and the airplane brought in people, too."

"The train depot was new when I left," I said. "But a lot has changed in ten years."

I was thinking about Bianca when I said it. Bianca all grown up with her beautiful big green eyes that sparkled like a Christmas morning.

"I guess so," she said. "Gradual changes. I notice little things every time I come back, but it's not jarring like it must be for you."

I smiled and, taking her coat from a peg near the back door, held it while she slipped into it. She pulls her gloves out of her pockets and slips them on.

"You forgot your hat," I said.

"Right." She felt her pockets. "I don't have it."

"Is this it?" I asked, picked up a gray wool cap from one of the shelves.

"That's it." She held out a hand. "I guess it fell out."

"Let me do it," I said.

She stood still while I placed the cap on her head. Adjusted her hair.

Our gazes locked and her lips parted slightly.

She was so close. It was such a perfect moment for a kiss.

But I ran a hand over her cheek and took a step back.

It wasn't time yet.

She told me she had to "officially" break up with her boyfriend before she would kiss me again.

I didn't like it, but I respected it. I respected it a lot.

Outside, the air had an unexpected bite to it.

It wouldn't be long before the first snow would fall.

I was looking forward to it. I might have adapted to Christmas without snow, but it didn't take away the joy of it.

"What time do you want me at your Grandpa's house tomorrow with breakfast?"

"You're bringing breakfast?" Even I heard the joy in my voice.

"That's my job, right? To keep you in food and drink?"

"That's so sexist," I said.

"You know." She looked up at the full moon beaming down through the tree limbs. "Maybe it should offend me, but it doesn't. Should it?"

She was looking at me with so much innocence, it tugged at my heart.

"No," I said, taking her gloved hand in mine and slowing. "The only reason I agreed to what Jackson suggested... that you keep us in food and drink... was because I want you there. With me. If you want to bring breakfast or whatever, that's okay, too. But I don't care about that. I just want to be able to look up and see you."

I kissed the back of her gloved hand.

Then she surprised me. She went into my arms, wrapping her arms around my waist and resting her head against my chest.

I put my arms around her and just held her. She fit perfectly in my arms. Just as I'd known she would.

We were meant for each other.

Bianca was my soulmate.

On some level I'd always known it, but now it just right there in front of me. So obvious.

I just had to let her move at her own pace.

There was no hurry.

"Are you okay?" I asked softly.

"Yes... No... Yes... I just 'um...'" She pushed back. Shook her head. Attempted a smile. "It's nothing."

I took her hand and we walked in silence the rest of the way to her home.

Walking. Holding her hand. It was the most natural thing in the world.

Chipmunks scurried about in the fallen leaves and a bird, probably an owl, flew into the sky as we walked beneath where he or maybe she had been perched on a limb.

Our way was lit by a mix of moonlight and the soft glow of the little solar lights along the pathway.

As we followed the trail for a time along the river, I couldn't hear anything over the roar of the rushing water, but then a few minutes later, we were back in the hush of the forest again.

The lights were on at her family's house, first floor and second.

I walked her up the steps to the door and waited while she keyed in the code to unlock the door.

"Good night," she said.

I tugged on her hand to bring her close, kissing her on the forehead.

"Sweet dreams my little one," I said.

Then I held the door open and waited until she closed it behind her.

I was gone. A man tossed over the edge. Lured onto the rocks.

Bianca was my siren.

And I crashed willingly onto the rocks.

Thirty-Four

Bianca

I stood just inside the door for a few minutes, giving myself time to steady.

I couldn't say what had come over me. Such a rush of emotions that it nearly made my knees weak.

After making a wish at the wishing well in town, everything seemed to be going down the path I had wished it to.

It was not possible that it was that easy. If it took no more than tossing a coin into a fountain and making a wish, then everyone in the world would be happy.

It was not that easy.

And yet...

Hearing people talking in the kitchen, I darted up the

stairs to my room. I wasn't in the mood to talk to anyone right now.

I wanted to replay my day with Scott. To savor every moment again and again.

In my room, I shrugged out of my coat and tossed it over a chair along with my gloves and hat.

When I'd been younger, I hadn't dared to entertain romantic thoughts of my brother's best friend. Well. Maybe a little. But he had seemed so not interested in me.

But now... Now he seemed totally into me.

I didn't understand it.

Was he just toying with me because he was here and I was here? Alpine Falls was just a stopover for him on his way to Arizona for Christmas.

Once he got his grandfather's house in order, he would move on.

There was nothing here in Alpine Falls to keep him.

So why was he acting more like a boyfriend than any boyfriend I'd ever had?

Boyfriend.

I looked at my phone. No messages.

I told him I needed to *break up* with Bradley before I kissed him again.

But was there anything to break up? Really?

Maybe my relationship with Bradley wasn't what I thought it was.

He obviously wasn't interested enough in me to stay in touch. He hadn't even asked how I was doing.

If I even made it here okay.

With or without Scott, my relationship with Bradley was over and I knew it.

Going to the window, I leaned my forehead against the icy cold glass and looked out toward the lodge.

I could just barely see a hint of smoke coming from the lodge's chimneys from here.

Scott was out there walking somewhere between here and the lodge. Headed back.

I'd wanted him to kiss me again. More than anything.

But I was the one who had made the no kissing until I'd officially broken up with Bradley rule.

At the time it had seemed like the proper thing to do.

And it was. I still believed that it was the proper thing to do.

And yet...

I couldn't think about anything other than Scott.

As I got ready for bed, I replayed our kiss. Our hug. Our trip into town.

I even replayed our trip into the attic.

He was the only person who could have gotten me to go into the attic at night.

The only one.

I would not have gone into that attic at night with anyone else.

But I had been safe and nothing had happened. I hadn't really expected it to, but still.

Unless we counted the flickering candles. Which I really didn't.

I could deal with some flickering candles, but if I saw a

full-fledged ghost standing in front of me, then that would be a different thing entirely.

I was about to turn away when a movement outside caught my attention.

At first I thought it might be Scott, coming around to see me once before he walked back.

A ludicrous thought, I knew, even as it formed.

But it wasn't Scott.

It was a couple walking hand in hand.

I started to turn away, but something pulled at me to watch them.

They weren't dressed like most people being outside at night would be dressed. They weren't wearing coats.

He was wearing a dark suit, very formal, his hair styled short beneath an old-fashioned hat.

She was wearing a white dress. I pressed my forehead against the window again and studied them.

A flapper dress, I decided. Like the 1920s. And a little hat that went with her outfit.

They stopped in the moonlight just below my window in the open area.

He said something to her, making her laugh. I couldn't hear them. I just knew.

Then he swept her into a dance. A waltz.

Then after twirling her around, he took her into a dip.

When he kissed her, I felt it all the way down to my bones.

It was almost as though I was the one being kissed.

I was transfixed. Even if I wanted to look away, I couldn't.

My breath formed a circle of fog on the glass. I quickly wiped it away with my sleeve.

But the couple was gone.

Vanished.

I strained my eyes to see into the darkness surrounding the house, but I knew.

They had simply vanished.

Thirty-Five

Scott

Even before getting to my grandfather's house early the next morning, I was regretting my decision to do the work to make it presentable.

I should have just sent my mother the pictures with the house in the state of disrepair that it is and revisit the house in the spring.

But I didn't have the heart to do that.

I just couldn't.

It was freezing and the house had no heat, but Jackson would be here soon and we would get to work.

The delivery truck, an old pickup truck, from the General Store pulled up and I helped the young man unload my supplies, stacking and organizing them neatly along the front porch.

"You gonna do all this work by yourself?" the young man asked me.

"No. My friend will be here shortly."

"Just call the General Store if you need some help. It looks like you're gonna need it."

"Thanks," I said. "Will do."

I wouldn't call him, but I appreciated the offer. Sort of. On the other hand, it told me that this really was an outlandish endeavor for two men.

And yet if anyone could do it, I was confident that Jackson and I could do it.

We'd take care of the outside of the house, the front first, then move to the inside.

Ready to get started, I located a scraper and went to work scraping off flakes of paint. Needless to say, there was a lot of loose paint. I moved methodically, left to right. Top to bottom. It was easy to see where I stopped each time.

After this, I would start sanding the wood. Sand. Then prime.

I knew my way around some construction work. Working part-time for a contractor during college had helped to offset some of the fees required to get an aviation degree.

I'd never looked it up, but I was pretty sure aviation had to be one of the most expensive college degrees to get. Aircraft rental. Instructor fees.

Worth every penny as far as I was concerned. I'd paid off

my college debt two years after graduation. Having the part-time job had helped.

And now that experience was helping me in spades.

Stopping to clean my scraper, I glanced toward the road.

I'd already been watching the road, but this time I was rewarded.

A newer model SUV pulled into the driveway and Bianca stepped out.

Going around to the passenger side, she pulled out a bag and a little cardboard cup holder.

I reached the bottom of the stairs in time to take the bag from her hands.

"Thank you," she said.

"This is heavy. What's in here?"

"I asked the cook, Wyndal... you might remember him... to put together a breakfast for us and I think he might have gone a little bit overboard."

"I do remember Wyndal." I set the bag on one of the boxes of supplies. "We'd go inside, but it's actually colder inside than it is out here."

"That's unfortunate," Bianca said, handing me a latte. "Why didn't you make a fire pit?"

"Because I didn't think about it." I sipped the smooth caramel latte. "Is that allowed?"

"If it's your property, you can do pretty much anything you want to."

"I'm not used to that. But." I glanced up toward the sky. "It's going to be a clear sunny day today so I think we'll warm up after we start working. And, yes, I looked at the weather report."

"I checked it, too," she said with a smile as she pulled three to go plates out of the bag. Handed me one.

They were still warm.

"He didn't have to do all this."

"It's okay. He didn't mind." She didn't open her own plate. Just sat and held it. "I thought Jackson was coming early."

"He'll be here. We should go ahead and eat," I said. "While it's hot."

"You're probably right." She took the plastic lid off her plate. Picked up a piece of crunchy bacon and took a bite.

She seemed a little bit distracted. I didn't know her well enough to know if she was a morning person.

"Are you okay?" I asked.

"Yeah. I'm okay," she said, shifting her plate in her lap.

It didn't seem right. Making her eat out here in the cold, holding her plate on her lap.

"You could have eaten at the lodge," I said.

"Trying to get rid of me already?"

"I was just thinking how much warmer and comfortable it is there."

"It's all about the experience," she said.

"Right," I said on a little laugh. "We can tell our grandchildren about it."

Bianca froze, looking at me with her big green eyes.

Thirty-Six

Bianca

It was just an expression. Something people said.

We'll tell our grandchildren about it.

He didn't mean OUR grandchildren. Just our respective grandchildren. His grandchildren and my grandchildren. Two different sets.

Still. Hearing him say those words so easily let loose a bevy of drunken butterflies in my stomach.

He glanced at me with a little impish grin, then just kept eating.

I narrowed my eyes at him, but he seemed completely unperturbed. Or maybe he was simply clueless.

I had almost forgotten that he was a nerd in high school and like my brother, Jackson, I had never known him to date in high school.

Picking up my coffee cup, I held it close, but my gloves were too thick to allow any heat from the hot coffee to get through.

He seemed quite cheerful for such an early, cold morning.

I could do mornings and often did, but getting out in the cold like this to have breakfast on the front porch of an abandoned house was most definitely a new experience.

Even my nose was cold.

A car drove slowly past. Scott and I both held up a hand to wave, even though we didn't know who the car belonged to.

It didn't really matter.

"Nobody waves in Denver," I mused.

"They wave in Houston," Scott said. "I mean. Not everybody. But there are friendly undertones to it that remind me of here."

"Alpine Falls isn't like most towns in the west." I took a sip of my coffee, then carefully set it down and picked up my fork.

"I think it's because it's so small. Everybody knows everybody."

"And their business."

"And that is another thing I like about Houston. Nobody cares what anyone else does."

"Friendly anonymity," I said. "There should be a word for that."

"I think you just coined it."

"Maybe pseudonymity."

"You just make this stuff up as you go, don't you?" he said with a little wink at me.

My breath hitched with that little wink and it took me a second to find my voice.

"You say that like it's a bad thing."

"There's nothing bad about it. It takes skill and talent. I'm actually quite impressed."

I knew we were sitting here, as we ate eggs and bacon and biscuits, talking about nothing at all, and yet I was still flustered to get such a compliment from Scott.

I was still getting used to the idea that he was sort of interested in me. In whatever way that was. A way that was as yet to be determined even though he had kissed me.

That kiss had changed things. Had upset my ecosystem.

I thought about telling him what I'd seen last night. It was right there on the tip of my tongue to tell him about the woman and the man walking in the moonlight. How he had swept her into a dance.

And then he had kissed her.

I put the back of my hand against my lips and looked over at Scott from beneath my eyelashes.

I'd been thinking about Scott when I'd seen the couple.

That had to be the only explanation for why I'd *felt* him kiss her.

As I was still debating *when* to tell Scott—I knew I would tell him, it was just a matter of when—my brother Jackson turned into the driveway in the family's old blue pickup truck.

I was saved from torturing myself about when to tell him by my brother showing up.

Thirty-Seven

Scott

The morning had passed by quickly. We'd taken a quick break for lunch, then got back to work.

We'd gotten a lot done. All the walls scraped and sanded. The debris from the yard bagged and placed out front by the road for pickup. Windows were newly scrubbed.

The house was already looking better. Part of that was probably from the way the sunlight reflected off the freshly cleaned windows.

It made a big difference, but I was ready to start painting. A fresh coat of paint was the thing that would really make the house glow.

Just as I had wished, Bianca was there any time I looked up from whatever I was doing.

The only time she'd left was to go get lunch.

I hadn't planned on her doing any work, but she was a Flynn and God help any man who tried to keep a Flynn from working when there was work to be done.

At the moment, she already had a can of paint opened up and was rolling paint over one of the shutters she'd had Jackson remove and place over a couple of sawhorses.

Her hair pulled back in a ponytail, she was wearing an Alpine Falls baseball cap. Her sweatshirt tied around her waist, she was wearing a long-sleeved t-shirt beneath it.

Jackson was on the other end of the house, still taking down shutters and stacking them near the sawhorses for Bianca. He was wearing air pods, but Bianca, like me, worked in silence.

She looked up, saw me watching her, and smiled before turning her attention back to her work.

I owed her dinner. Both of them. Bianca and Jackson.

Finished stirring the can of white paint, I poured some into a pan. The fresh scent of paint filled the air and that first swipe of white onto the newly sanded wall gave me a glimpse of how much better the house was going to look with fresh paint. There was nothing like a fresh coat of paint to make a house look a hundred percent better.

It would have been easier to just hire someone to do this, but no one wanted to work a big job like this at Christmastime. Our goal was to just make sure the pictures didn't shock my mother too terribly bad.

As I painted the wall near the door, the sunshine warm on my back, humming a catchy Christmas song to myself, I lost track of time.

"You 'bout ready to call it a day?" Jackson asked, coming up to stand next to me.

I glanced at my watch and looked up. Bianca stood a few feet behind him. She was wearing her sweatshirt now and looked ready to go.

I glanced at my watch a second time. I hadn't realized so much time had passed.

I'd been thinking about my grandfather, worrying about his condition. Worrying about what we were going to do about his house—this house. Worried that it was going to fall on my shoulders.

"It's time to call it a day," I said. "Time got away."

Jackson started cleaning everything up. Pouring paint back into the can. Gathering up my roller and putting it in a plastic crate to take back to his house to clean up since there was no running water here.

With all the worrying I'd been doing, with all the worry settled onto my shoulders, I was surprised that when my gaze settled on Bianca just how quickly that worry faded away.

She had that effect on me. A calming effect.

Just a glance at her told me that everything was going to work out.

I didn't have to know how, but I knew it would.

Thirty-Eight

Bianca

The sun was down for the night, taking its warmth with it.

After a hot shower and a much needed change of clothes, I left my bedroom and headed downstairs.

The plan was to meet Jackson and walk over to the lodge with him to have dinner with Scott.

Scott felt beholden to us for helping him out with the house. I hadn't minded. It was nice to get out in the fresh air and get a little exercise.

He didn't have to buy us dinner, but I wanted to spend time with him.

I was getting used to having him around.

To his credit, Jackson hadn't asked anything about why

the two of us seemed to suddenly be talking and hanging out.

I still caught him watching us now and then with obvious questions in his eyes, but he kept them to himself.

When I reached the first floor, I went back to the kitchen to get a drink of water.

Jackson was already there.

"Hey," I said. "Are we walking or driving?"

"Driving," he said. "I'm bringing Tabitha back after dinner."

"Okay." Ready to go now, I put on my coat and gloves.

We headed out the back and climbed into the old truck. To his credit, Jackson already had the truck running and warmed up.

"You're a good brother," I said, holding my hands in the warm air coming out of the vents.

He backed out of the driveway.

"So," he said. "What's up with you and Scott?"

So much for him not saying anything.

"What do you mean?" I asked, batting my lashes innocently.

Jackson just rolled his eyes. "You know what I mean."

"I don't know," I said, serious now. "It's like we've known each other forever. And yet we know so little about each other."

"You have known each other forever," he said.

"But we never once talked. Not really."

"Still," he said. "There's that familiarity."

"I guess that's it."

He pulled out onto the lane that curved around toward the lodge. A flock of birds left the trees heading toward the sky.

"You like him," he said. It wasn't a question. Just a simple statement.

I could deny it. But why?

What good would it do to deny something that was so real? So special?

And yet something that couldn't possibly go anywhere.

"You haven't kept up with him?" I asked instead of answering. "Why?"

"No reason in particular. We just both got busy doing our own things."

"So nothing happened?"

"Nope. We're still good friends as far as I'm concerned."

"It's so weird how guys can do that."

"It's a gift," Jackson said.

I smiled. "I can see why the two of you were such good friends. Are such good friends."

"He's a good guy. Always has been."

Jackson pulled into a parking spot in the back lot of the lodge and put the truck in park.

"He lives in Houston," I said.

"And you live in Denver," Jackson said.

"It can't go anywhere," I said, putting words to the very thing that had been troubling me from the very beginning.

Jackson looked over at me with blue eyes that mirrored mine expect in color.

"If something is meant to be, it'll be," he said. "I honestly don't even think we have much control over it."

"That's rather fatalistic," I said wryly.

He shrugged. "Not meant to be. I actually see it as a good thing."

"How can that possibly be a good thing?"

An older woman with her dog came out the back door, saw us, and held up a hand in a wave. We both waved back.

"It means we don't have to try so hard. Just be yourself and things will work out the way they're supposed to."

"How did you get to be so wise?" I asked.

I was supposed to be the psychologist here, but my brother was giving me words of wisdom.

"It's easy for me to say because I'm not in it."

"True," I said. "But how do we know what's meant to be?"

"I guess it's what feel right," he said. "Come on. We're gonna be late."

We got out of the truck and started walking toward the lodge in the moonlight.

Glancing up toward the attic, a movement caught my eye.

A woman stood there watching us. At first she just looked like a shape, but then as we moved closer, I could make out more.

I put a hand over my mouth to stifle a gasp and I my feet froze to the ground.

It was her. The woman I'd seen outside my window last night in the moonlight.

"What is it?" Jackson asked, taking a step back toward me.

I glanced at him for just the briefest of moments.

"It's..." I looked up again, but the window was just dark. I couldn't see anything. "Nothing," I said. "A trick of the light."

Jackson looked at me with obvious skepticism, but didn't press me for more information.

Instead the two of us walked the rest of the way together, in silence, and went in through the back door into the warmth of the lodge.

I couldn't explain what was happening. Why I kept seeing what I feared was Abigail, but I also didn't know who to confide in.

My sister Arabella came to mind since she had supposedly seen Abigail, but oddly enough that was the very reason I was reluctant to talk to her.

Arabella would already have an iron-clad opinion about Abigail and ghosts. I wasn't sure I was ready to hear that.

I sort of wanted to figure it out for myself.

Or... maybe what I really wanted to do was to talk to Scott about it.

I just wasn't so sure he was ready to hear it.

Thirty-Nine

Scott

After getting cleaned up and putting on some clean clothes, I left my room and headed down the second-floor hallway of the lodge.

The candles in the sconces were flickering.

I stopped and watched them.

First of all, there was no wind. No breeze.

Second of all, even if there was a breeze, the flames were behind glass globes. There was no way they could be affected by any such breeze. If there had been one.

Just as I had done when Bianca challenged me, I walked over to the nearest sconce and lifted the globe.

The flame immediately stopped flickering.

"Now, that's weird," I said.

I pulled the candle from its seat and stretched up to my full height to see into the empty candle holder. There was nothing there. No trigger that released when the candle was lifted.

Just to test it, I put the candle back and counted to ten, but the flickering didn't start back again.

I replaced the globe and after scratching my chin, continued down the hallway.

Maybe the lodge was just old. Weird things happened in old buildings like this. Maybe there was some kind of draft coming from the ceiling that caused the candles to flicker.

Whatever it was, I didn't need to worry about it right now.

Right now, I was about to have dinner with my best friend and his sister.

Or maybe I should say I was about to have dinner with my girl and her brother.

There. I liked that better.

Bianca was my girl.

It was just that I was currently the only person who knew that.

Even she didn't know that.

I found them, Bianca and Jackson, already seated at a booth in the lounge.

Bianca's hair was down, flowing softly around her shoulders. Her pink bow-shaped lips sparkled with something glittery and glossy.

She immediately scooted over when she saw me. I slid into the booth next to her.

"You clean up nice," Jackson told me.

"You too." I told him, then winked at Bianca.

"It's just good to get together," Jackson said. "to catch up."

"It's been too long coming," I said.

The server, a young lady I didn't recognize—probably just a kid when I'd lived here before—stopped and took our drink order.

Bianca was staring out the window looking out over the lobby.

"How's life in the big city of Houston?"

"Getting plenty of flying hours in. Same for you in Denver?"

"I stay busy."

The server dropped our drinks off. A sparkling water for Bianca. Bottles of beer for me and Jackson.

"You must get back here a lot," I said.

"Not nearly as much as my mother would like."

"I know what you mean."

Another glance at Bianca. She was still staring out the window as though she was watching for someone.

"I need to take this call," Jackson said, pulling his phone out of his pocket. "I'll be back in a minute."

"Are you okay?" I asked Bianca. "Watching for someone?"

"No," she said, twisting in her seat to face me.

"You seem like something's bothering you," I said.

"No," she said again, lowering her gaze.

Despite her protests, I knew something was bothering her. She just wasn't ready to talk about it yet.

"Did something happen?" I asked. I wanted to find out what was bothering her away and wipe it away. Instead of seeing her troubled, I wanted to see her smile.

She looked up, meeting my gaze.

"I thought I saw something," she said softly.

I glanced over her head. "Where? In the lobby?"

"No," she said. "In the attic window."

Forty

Bianca

Christmas music spilled from hidden speakers blending with conversations in the crowded lounge.

I was sitting in a booth pressed against the glass wall, giving me a good view of the lobby. Scott sat on my other side. He smelled good. Like a blue spruce after a rain shower.

A beer from a frosted bottle sat on the table in front of him, dripping with condensation.

Jackson had walked off to answer a phone call, leaving me alone with Scott.

Scott, in that astute way of his, seemed to notice that I was troubled by something.

Then, once I started talking about it, I didn't seem to be able to stop.

"I saw someone standing in the attic window with a light behind her. But when I glanced away for just less than a second, not even a second, she was gone and the window was dark.

"Has that happened before?" he asked, twirling his bottle.

"No. Never. But..."

He turned, resting an elbow on the table, picking up his beer with his other hand.

"But?"

"Last night when I was standing at my window I saw someone. A couple. Walking by, hand in hand. They stopped right beneath my window and started dancing."

"Dancing?"

"Yeah. Waltzing. And they looked like they were from another time. Another era."

I barely took a breath and kept going.

"They were wearing hats. You know. Formal hats. Dressy."

He was looking at me like he had no idea what I was talking about.

"Wait." I opened up my phone. Did a quick google search. Held up a picture for him. "Like this."

"Oooh." He sat back. Looked at me. "That's a little strange."

"I know."

"What do you make of it?"

"I don't know what to make of it."

"Maybe it's Abigail."

I shivered. That was exactly what I had been thinking.

"I hope not," I said. "Maybe it was just a couple of guests out for a walk."

"It's possible."

I set my phone aside. "That's right. That's all it was. Just a couple of guests in the moonlight."

The server came back about the time Jackson returned from his phone call.

"Everything okay?" Scott asked.

"Just a business thing," Jackson said. "Nothing to worry about."

He looked from one of us to the other.

"What did I miss?"

"Nothing," we both said at the same time.

"Nothing. Right."

The server took our order.

"How much do you think we have left to do over at your grandpa's house?" Jackson asked, seeing that we didn't want to tell about whatever it was we'd been talking about.

"I think just one more day. Tomorrow. And we'll have everything photo ready."

Jackson smiled. "I hope she appreciates everything."

"To be honest with you," Scott said. "I hope she never finds out just how bad it was."

As they talked more about options for the house, my thoughts wandered back to the girl I had seen in the attic window and the couple outside my window last night.

I'd only seen a glimpse of the girl in the window, but I was pretty sure it was the same girl I'd seen last night waltzing in the moonlight.

I didn't know what it meant that I was suddenly seeing what could only be ghosts.

I'd grown up here and in all those years I had managed to avoid seeing anything that resembled a ghost, even though I'd heard about a ghost named Abigail.

And now I had a pretty good feeling I had seen her. And a guy. No one had ever mentioned a guy.

So now I had seen not only the ghost known as Abigail, but a male ghost that no one had ever mentioned.

Scott seemed a little bit surprised by it, but he wasn't nearly as disconcerted as I was.

After all, I was the one who had seen them.

And besides, Scott wasn't afraid of anything. Whatever it was, he just wanted to figure it out.

I didn't necessarily want to figure it out. I just wanted to know what it meant.

It had to mean something.

Forty-One

Scott

After dinner, Jackson checked his watch.

"I'm supposed to give Tabitha a ride home. You coming, Bianca?"

She looked at him a moment, then glanced over at me.

I could tell she was fading. It had been a long day.

"I need to head up to my room. Get some sleep," I said. "Tomorrow's going to be another long day."

I stood up and held out a hand to help Bianca slide out of the booth.

"I'll go start the truck," Jackson said. "Get it warmed up."

"I'll be right out," Bianca said. "Don't leave without me."

After Jackson left to go start the truck, I held Bianca's coat while she slid into it.

All bundled up, she looked at me with her big green eyes and I realized I wasn't ready to let her go.

"I'll walk you out to the truck," I said, sliding into my own coat.

"You don't have to do that."

"Trying to get rid of me?" I asked.

"No," she said. "I'm not trying to get rid of you."

I held out an arm for her. She slid her arm into the crook of my elbow and together we walked out into the lobby.

Half a dozen trees, about six feet tall each, stood at various points around the lobby, people busy draping them with garland and balls and beads.

"I forgot about the decorating contest," she said.

"It looks like Arabella has it under control." And it did. Arabella walked around from group to group. Giving suggestions. Solving problems. Doing what she obviously loved doing best. Managing.

"I should probably offer to help her," Bianca said.

"Probably," I said, but I kept walking, not giving her a chance to make a detour.

She worked too hard.

"But you've got a busy day ahead of yourself tomorrow. After a busy day today."

"True."

We stepped outside into the cool night air that smelled suspiciously like snow.

If the weather forecasters were correct, and I agreed with their assessment, it wasn't going to snow tonight. Maybe tomorrow night. Definitely by Christmas.

Still. The air had the feel of snow to it.

Tabitha and Jackson were already in the truck, waiting for Bianca.

I opened the door and helped Bianca climb inside.

"Scott?" Jackson said before I could close the door. "You have a few minutes? Hop in. I need to ask you about something."

"Sure." I didn't even hesitate. The girls slid over, giving me room to sit on the bench with them.

I didn't have to be offered twice the chance to ride, however short a ride it was, next to Bianca. Putting my arm around her shoulders, I held her close as Jackson turned out of the parking lot onto the road leading to the Flynn manor.

If anyone asked about my intentions, I was merely keeping her safe. There were, after all, no seatbelts in the old trucks.

I'd take any excuse I could to be close to Bianca Flynn.

Forty-Two

Bianca

I was up early the next morning and on my way into town before the sun had time to burn off the fog that hovered over the ground.

The coffee shop was already filled with people getting their early morning cup of coffee before they headed into the shops for work or for shopping.

It was, after all, just three days until Christmas. It was going to be busy and crowded every day between now and then.

I loved it.

These couple of days leading up to Christmas Eve were my favorite time of year. They carried a kind of magic.

A promise that anything was possible.

It was a feeling I hoped never faded, even when I was older and had children of my own.

"Good morning, Bianca," the barista smiled. "Same as yesterday?"

"Yes, actually," I said. "You remember?"

"Yes ma'am." The college student grinned. "I have a good memory. How are the renovations coming?"

"Just fine," I said. It didn't pay to act surprised. In a town the size of Alpine Falls, everybody knew everybody and everybody's business along with it, especially when anyone did anything out of the ordinary. Painting the outside of a house and doing various other renovations at Christmastime was definitely out of the ordinary. "We're making real progress."

The barista got to work on our coffee.

"How do you think you're going to like living there?" she asked.

"Excuse me?"

"Living there. In town. How do you think you'll like living there?"

"I'm not... I don't... I don't understand." I tried to smile. The young lady was obviously confused.

She handed me one cup of coffee and got to work on the next one.

"I heard you and Scott Brooks were getting married and moving in there together."

"Where on earth did you hear something like that?" I asked, feeling my cheeks pinken.

"Mr. Creek came in. Said he'd heard it from Mr. Miller who heard it from your grandfather's neighbor."

"And they say women like to gossip," I said, stepping aside to clear the line.

"Scott Brooks is a looker," she said as she packed up the three cups in a cardboard carrier. "Everyone's happy for you."

"I see," I said. Who was I to disappoint everyone in town? Besides, I knew from experience that even if I tried to deny it, she wouldn't believe me. Such was the power of the Alpine Falls gossip mill.

Five minutes later I pulled into Scott's Grandpa's driveway and went around to get out the breakfast.

"Let me get that for you," Scott said, hurrying forward to grab the bag of food.

"If I didn't know better," I said. "I'd think you'd been watching for me."

"What man could resist a breakfast like this? And coffee too?"

I rolled my eyes at him just as my brother rumbled up in his old truck, pulling into the driveway next to my car.

"I made it in time for a hot breakfast today," Jackson said.

"Men are simple creatures," Scott said. "Easily motivated."

"I refuse to comment on that," I said, unpacking the coffee cups.

"I stopped for gas and guess what I heard," Jackson said.

"What did you hear?" Scott asked, unpacking the hot breakfast.

"I heard you two are getting married and moving in here," he said. "You know you could have told me, right?"

Scott's hands stilled on the plate he was pulling for just a moment, but I must have imagined it. "I heard that two days ago," he said, dismissively.

"I heard the same thing at the coffee shop this morning," I said, looking across the fence toward the neighbor's house. "Seems the neighbors have been making up gossip."

"You could do worse for yourself," Jackson said.

I balled up a napkin and threw it at him.

"Thanks," he said, catching it easily and uncrumpling it, then making a show of dabbing his mouth with it.

Scott was watching us with amusement.

"Why is no one concerned about this?" I wondered, taking the plastic lid off my plate.

Scott and Jackson just laughed.

"It's harmless gossip," Jackson said. "Neither one of you live here. They'll see soon enough just how wrong they are."

I took a swallow of coffee and fought down a sick feeling.

That was the problem.

The guys were blowing this off like it wasn't the least bit important.

But they hadn't stopped to consider that it did mean something to me.

And maybe, just maybe, I wanted them to take it at least a little bit seriously.

Because for me it was serious.

Like my brother had said in jest, I could do a lot worse.

Forty-Three

Scott

As I rolled what was a second coat of paint over the far wall, I considered what the rumor mill had been up to.

I hadn't actually heard the rumor that Bianca and I were getting married and moving in here, but I didn't want to make a big deal out it.

I only said I'd heard it two days ago to show how ridiculous the whole thing was. Two days ago, we weren't even working on the house.

Bianca had finished the shutters and was meticulously painting the narrow porch rails. Some of them needed to be replaced, but that was a job for another day.

Right now we were going above and beyond my original

intent. But then I hadn't known I would have help. Having help was an unexpected surprise. Especially for that help to include Bianca.

It was nice to look up whenever I wanted to. To smile at her and get a smile in return.

I couldn't think of anything nicer.

Except maybe for what I had wished for at the wishing well.

That would be nicer.

But this was most definitely a step in that direction.

We'd be finished with the outside today and tomorrow I would take a look at what needed to be done inside. I wasn't as worried about the inside as I had been about the outside.

My mother would be worried about appearances and the outside of the house was a definite indicator of appearances. She couldn't help it. Like me, she'd been born and raised here, but unlike me, she'd spent most of her adult life here, too.

I suppose that indoctrinated a person into the culture of a town.

I think it was also, maybe more importantly, an indication of my grandfather's state of mind when he left Alpine Falls.

It was interesting how my good deed had gone from doing something good for my mother to doing something for myself.

The townspeople were going to draw their own conclusions no matter what.

There was nothing anyone could do about that.

It wasn't like what they were saying was a bad thing.

As strange as it was, I could actually see myself living here with Bianca.

For me to see myself living in Alpine Falls to begin with was shocking enough to begin with.

When I'd left here, I hadn't exactly shaken the dirt of Alpine Falls off my feet, but when my parents moved to Arizona, I'd had no need to come back here and honestly never thought I ever would.

But then to suddenly picture myself living here with Bianca, was definitely unexpected.

What was I supposed to do with that?

Bianca didn't live here. I didn't live here.

We didn't live here.

There was no *we*.

No matter how much I might wish for there to be a *we*, there wasn't.

At least not yet.

I glanced back over at her sitting comfortably on the porch, patiently drawing a streak of white paint down one side of a skinny rail, then the next side.

She was relaxed, her lips parted ever so slightly.

Her baseball cap lay next to her and the bright morning sunlight glinted off her hair, revealing the subtle highlights I hadn't noticed before. A lock of hair escaped her ponytail, falling across her cheek.

The highlights were a not so subtle reminder that Bianca might be from here, but she no longer lived here.

This was no longer her world.

She was a professional psychologist, a university professor, spending her time sitting here painting my grandfather's
porch railings.

Was I taking advantage of her kindness?

Frowning as I rolled my paint roller in a tray of fresh
paint and took it back to the wall, I considered that
possibility.

Anyone else besides Bianca, I might think just that.

But no. I wasn't taking advantage of her.

I *liked* her.

I *liked* her a lot.

More than I had ever liked anyone else.

It was as though my emotions had been lying dormant
just waiting for Bianca to come back into my life.

But how was I supposed to translate the emotions I was
feeling for her into something more than mere emotions?

She had her career and I had mine.

And other than this unexpected interlude in Alpine
Falls, our paths did not cross.

She lived in Denver and came here often.

I lived in Houston and never came to Alpine Falls. When
I went home for the holidays, home was now in Arizona.

There was no intersection of our lives and I couldn't
foresee one.

Forty-Four

Bianca

I paced my bedroom as I contemplated the text message on my phone.

It was from Bradley.

It just sat there, begging for a reply.

I didn't have one.

No. That wasn't true. I had several.

I had several replies, but I wasn't sure just which one I wanted to send.

What took you so long?

I'm not sure I want you to come after all.

Please don't come.

So I pace some more and don't respond.

So much had changed since last Friday afternoon when I had left Denver feeling disappointed as I drove myself to Alpine Falls.

I was supposed to have been coming here with my boyfriend, but instead I came by myself.

I stopped at the window and looked down to where I had seen the couple dancing in the moonlight just last night.

So very much had changed.

I didn't even feel like the same person as I had been when I had packed up my car and left the city.

I didn't feel like the girl I'd been when I'd grown up here either.

It was odd.

I wasn't in my past, exactly, and I wasn't in my present.

I felt like I was in some kind of fantasy world. A world where time folded up on itself and was neither the past nor the future. I was simply here in the present.

In a new kind of present. Maybe it was an alternate reality.

I shook my head. I was being fanciful.

My head was full of images of Scott.

Scott perched on a ladder rolling paint on the side of his grandfather's house. He was only painting his grandfather's house to save his mother's feelings.

He didn't want her to see the state of disrepair her father

had left it in when he had gotten in his car and driven to Arizona to live with her.

From all accounts, he had some kind of dementia. Perhaps the state of the house spoke to his state of mind when he left the house.

I walked away from the window.

Images of Scott kneeling next to me in the attic going through trunks and boxes searching for old, but not sentimental, Christmas decorations.

Images of Scott sitting next to me eating vanilla (and chocolate) ice cream.

I sat down at my vanity and picked up a hairbrush. Ran it through my hair.

Scott was a pilot for Skye Travels and I would do well not to fall for him.

But any woman in her right mind could see that it was too late.

I'd fallen for Scott Brooks when I'd been a teenager. He'd been a year older. My brother's best friend and he'd never given me a second look.

He'd watched me sometimes, but I always just figured he was curious about me because I was Scott's little sister. I was probably doing something he thought was silly at the time.

That was, at least, what I had thought at the time.

Perhaps I had been mistaken. Maybe... just maybe... there had been more to his curious glances than I had thought.

A girl could hope.

Ready now, I sent a response to Bradley's text message.

Forty-Five

Scott

Before leaving Grandpa's house for the evening, I snapped a few pictures of the outside of the house with my phone.

I waited until I was back in my room, though, before I sent them to my mother. I had my reasons and it turned out I was right on the mark.

It wasn't five minutes before my phone rang.

"Hi Mom," I said.

"Scott," she said. "The house looks so much better than I expected it to."

"I was a little surprised, too." I paced across the bedroom, the phone pressed against my ear.

"Come home," she said. "You've been there long enough."

"Don't you want me to check out the inside?" My stomach dropped. "Take some pictures?"

"No," she said. "That's not necessary. It's been a year since you were home." She took what sounded like a deep breath. "Come home. For Christmas."

"I stopped by last summer," I said.

"It was an overnight stay. For work."

There was something in her voice that told me something was bothering her.

"What's wrong, Mom?" I asked.

"Is it wrong to want my son to come home for Christmas?"

I lowered the phone a moment. My mother rarely used guilt on me, but when she did, she pulled out all the stops.

"Is Marianne coming home?" I asked.

"No," Mom said. "She's staying in Pennsylvania with her husband's family."

"Ah," I said. That explained it. That explained why she wanted me home. My sister wasn't coming home and she wanted at least one of her two children home for Christmas.

I stopped and stared out the window into the moonlight. It made me think of what Bianca had told me about seeing a couple dancing in the moonlight. They had been there, then just as quickly, they had vanished.

Although I peered out into the moonlight, I wasn't fortunate enough to see such an unusual sight.

I wasn't ready to go home.

I wasn't ready to leave Bianca.

She and I hadn't gotten anything worked out. We hadn't even talked about seeing each other again, much less talked about how we might stay in touch with each other after going back to our respective cities.

My mother sniffled. She actually sniffled. "Christmas won't be the same without at least one of my children home. And your grandfather isn't getting any younger. He keeps asking about you."

I groaned to myself. She was really laying on the guilt tonight.

Maybe I needed to head down to Arizona to see what was going on down there.

"I'm a little busy," I said. "with work. I can make plans to come in two or three weeks." In two or three weeks, Bianca would be back at work in Denver and I wouldn't be leaving her here.

Mother didn't say anything for a moment. Usually I heard Grandpa talking in the background. Anytime she got on the phone, he liked to jump in there and be part of a conversation he could only hear half of.

"It's quiet there," I said. "Where is everyone?"

"Your father is at work and Grandpa is taking a nap."

"You must be enjoying the moment of quietness," I said, at a loss as to what else to say.

"It's a little unusual." I heard the genuine sadness in her voice now.

"Okay," I said, running a hand through my hair and

although I don't know why, I glanced at my watch. "I can fly down, but I need to come right back."

I could practically hear the smile spread across her face. "That's wonderful. I'll make an apple pie."

Despite my reluctance to leave Alpine Falls just yet, I knew that was exactly what I was about to do.

Forty-Six

Bianca

The next morning, Mother kept me home helping her with some last minute gift wrapping. I think it was just an excuse for her to spend time with me, but I could hardly claim that I needed to get over to the lodge on the outside chance I could run into Scott.

Scott and I didn't have any plans for today. He hadn't decided what he was going to do about the inside of house. Jackson had suggested that he just come clean with his mother and tell her that the house was in a state of disrepair.

Scott wanted to think about it. I didn't blame him. He didn't see his family often so it was natural that he wanted to please them, especially his mother.

After we got all the gifts wrapped and put under the tree, Mother wanted to have lunch so we ate tuna sandwiches and potato chips in her sunroom.

There wasn't much sun, but the way the clouds clung to the mountain peaks made a postcard ready picture.

It looked cold and dreary, but that's how it was supposed to look in December. The cold and dreary always came before the snowfall.

After lunch, Mother headed up to her bedroom to take a nap giving me time to walk over to the lodge.

Bundled in my coat, I took my time, walking slowly, enjoying the quietness and calmness. Chipmunks darted out in front of me on the trail, then darted away just as quickly. Black birds swept down, looking for food. Prancing about expectantly. Hoping I'd brought some peanuts or some other treat for them.

I didn't, of course. Maybe next time I'd think about it. My grandmother used to put bird feeders out all year long, but no one seemed to have the patience or time to do anything like that anymore.

Somehow it seemed like the more technology we had at our fingertips, the less time we had to do things.

I went in through the backdoor of the lodge and hung my coat on one of the hooks near the door. I stuffed my gloves and hat in my coat pockets.

As I walked past the lounge, festive Christmas music spilled out, and I sang along in my head.

This was going to be the best Christmas ever.

I wandered past the large four-sided fireplace with its cozy warmth drifting out in all directions.

Guests had already settled in, making themselves comfortable in the oversized chairs surrounding the fireplace.

It reminded me of the textbook I needed to read and highlight. I'd barely touched it since I'd gotten here. There was still plenty of time. Classes didn't start until after the new year.

I'd been looking forward to getting ahead, but the time I'd spent with Scott was worth it. I wouldn't go back and change a thing.

In fact, if I buckled down the first week before classes started, I could still get ahead and stay ahead a week or so. It was enough. I'd taught personality psychology before, just from a different textbook.

I knew how to change my priorities when I needed to.

As I neared the front desk, Arabella and Zoe looked up. They both wore similar expressions when they saw me. A cross between concern and confusion.

"Hey," I said, trying to force a smile as I looked at them sideways. "Everything okay?"

Arabella and Zoe exchanged a glance.

"Everything is good," Arabella said. "Can you come back to the office for a minute?"

Something was wrong. It wasn't anything urgent, but it was something.

"Sure," I said, following my sister behind the desk to her office. "What's wrong?"

Arabella didn't bother to ask me to sit down. She knew better.

"Did you know that Scott checked out?" she asked.

"What?" My brain didn't... couldn't... register what she was saying. "Checked out? Of the lodge?"

"This morning. Early."

"But... why?"

"I don't know," Arabella said. "I wasn't here and it was before Zoe got here. Did you know he was planning on leaving today?"

"No." I slid into the nearest chair and Arabella sat in the chair next to mine.

"I didn't think so," she said, tucking a strand of hair behind an ear.

I felt a little faint. Like my ears were ringing.

Taking a deep breath, I forced myself to pull it together.

It didn't mean anything.

He was a pilot. He could have been called out to take a flight. People were always needing last minute, unexpected flights. I knew this. My brothers were pilots. Last minute flights were the pilot's way of life.

But he'd check out.

"He checked out," I said.

"I'm sure there's a good explanation," Arabella said. "I just didn't want to catch you off guard out there."

"Thank you," I said. Then. "I don't want to keep you from working."

"Got it," Arabella said, tapping me on the shoulder. "I'm here if you need anything."

She left but I didn't. I just sat there. Numb.

Scott hadn't said anything to me last night about leaving. Was that why he hadn't made plans with me for today?

My fingers closed around my phone. I didn't even have Scott's cell phone number and he didn't have mine.

If he'd left a note for me, Arabella would have told me.

He'd just up and left.

Maybe this wasn't going to be the best Christmas ever after all.

Scott

The morning clouds were heavy with impending snow poised to fall at any minute. The clouds that had been hanging around the tall mountain peaks had dropped into the valley, making the sky seem lower without a view of the mountains above them.

The air was chilly, making me thankful I wasn't trying to do any painting or yard work this morning.

It felt good to be back in the cockpit. Nonetheless, I flew out of Alpine Falls with a heavy heart.

I hadn't said anything to anyone about leaving. Not Jackson. And certainly not Bianca.

My plan was to slip out. Appease my mother and come right back.

By my estimation, I could be back in Alpine Falls by Christmas Eve.

I didn't have everything planned out yet, not the details anyway, but I had every intention of keeping what I thought of as a promise.

When I had told Bianca that I wouldn't leave her on Christmas, I had meant it.

Taking a page from Bianca's playbook, I had decided that it would be best to tell my parents in person that I wasn't going to be home for Christmas.

I would be there long enough to have apple pie and exchange gifts and do whatever other traditions Mother was intent on us keeping, but she would understand, she would have to understand that, like my sister, I had someone now who required me to stay with her family.

That first feeling of weightlessness that came when the plane first left the ground never got old. I made a circle over the lodge, looking all innocently asleep.

The way I figured it, my parents were going to have to start being flexible. They were going to have to start traveling for Christmas. My sister's in Pennsylvania and now me in Colorado.

I was getting a little ahead of myself, sure, but I was a proactive thinker.

All I had to do was to figure out how to go about convincing Bianca that she and I were meant to be together.

We'd been meant to be together since we'd been kids. I

couldn't pinpoint the exact time when I had first started crushing on her. It was just always the way it was.

It was that way before I even knew it.

I'd had a crush on Bianca before I even knew what a crush was.

My heart grew heavier the more miles I put between me and Bianca.

Then somewhere over the southeastern corner of Utah, I began to feel better. The sooner I got home and straightened everything out with my mother, the sooner I could get back to Alpine Falls.

I needed to get Bianca a Christmas present.

I glanced at my watch again, for no reason in particular.

Like most everyone I knew, I didn't wear a sports watch. I wore a real watch. A nice oyster band, ice blue dial, platinum casing.

And right there looking at my watch, I knew what that perfect gift was.

It was a little presumptuous, but I could be a presumptuous guy when I needed to be.

And when the woman of my dreams was on the line, presumptuousness was most definitely called for.

I knew what I needed to do.

Forty-Eight

Bianca

The next two days passed in a haze.

Everyone kept saying it was going to snow.

The clouds were white and heavy with it. It was almost like the clouds themselves were waiting for Christmas.

Every year my sister Arabella hosted a masquerade ball at the lodge. It had grown over the years into a destination party and only lodge guests were allowed.

It was quite an ordeal. Men wore tuxedos and women wore long elegant ballgowns, mostly in black, some in Christmas red, and a couple in deep green.

We served chocolate and caramel coated pecan balls, caviar, and champagne.

A five-piece orchestra played Christmas music and the lounge closed its doors.

That was Arabella's solution to getting the men out of the lounge and on the dance floor with their wives. Oddly enough, it worked.

I remembered when Arabella first started having the masquerade ball. Anyone in town was invited. There were still a few people in town who were invited, but they had to pay an entrance fee.

I had to give it to Arabella. She was a shrew businesswoman.

Although she hired people to do most of the prep, there was still a lot to do. So I spent Christmas Eve day helping her.

We had lists to check. Poinsettias and amaryllis arrangements to place. Chairs had to be moved about. Others brought in. A dozen helpers running around had to be directed and supervised. The preparation was quite the production.

About five o'clock, she looked over at me, her iPad held closed to her chest.

"Go get dressed," she said.

"When are you going to get dressed?" I asked, evading what was surely meant as a suggestion.

She glanced at her watch. "I'll be right behind you. Just a couple more things to do."

"Okay," I said. "I'll head back to the house."

I took my time putting on my coat, enjoying the orchestra music. But it was bittersweet.

Being here at the ball alone, was too painful. In the back of my mind, deep in my unconscious, I had been planning to attend with Scott.

The thought of attending the ball alone, without Scott, was not something I could bear. Maybe next year. Maybe next year I would feel better about the whole thing and I would have Scott out of my head.

But not now. Not this year.

The house would be empty so I was going to light a fire in the living room, open a bottle of champagne, and do absolutely nothing.

I never did nothing. I was always reading. Or studying. Or working on something.

But tonight, I decided, I was going to do nothing.

Then tomorrow, on Christmas Day, I would spend the day with my family. After that, I would start thinking about going back to Denver. Back in my own space, I would get some work done without watching the doors for Scott.

I hated it that I couldn't be in the lodge without glancing toward the door every three minutes. Hoping to see him stride through. Apologetic that he hadn't at the least left a note for me.

Bundled up, I walked home. Arabella wouldn't approve of me walking home in the early evening darkness alone, but I was glad I did.

Just as I reached the riverbank, the first snowflakes drifted down, landing on the sleeves of my coat.

I looked up and a snowflake landed on my eyelashes.

It made me smile in spite of myself. I smiled because Scott had gotten his wish.

He had wished for Christmas snow and here it was.

I hadn't gotten my wish, but that was okay. I'd wished for something outlandish on purpose. Just because I knew it wouldn't come true.

I figured I would go big or go home.

So I went big.

And now I was going home.

The rest of the walk in the moonlight with snowflakes drifting down slowly almost made me believe in the magic of Christmas again. Almost.

It was okay.

I was looking forward to my quiet Christmas Eve at home.

Doing nothing.

Forty-Nine

Scott

I had forgotten about the Alpine Lodge Masquerade Ball.

Only the Flynns would host a masquerade ball on Christmas Eve when most people were spending a quiet evening at home with their families.

Unfortunately I wasn't dressed appropriately to attend a formal ball. I had on my black slacks and white button-down shirt beneath my wool trench coat. I left my captain's cap in the airplane and walked the distance from the airport to the lounge dragging my suitcase behind me on the uneven packed dirt path.

Patting my pocket as I walked, I figured I could be in and

out before the party started. Or... perhaps even better, I could change into my tuxedo and show up at the ball.

I actually stopped at the fork in the path. If I turned left, I'd go straight to the Flynn Manor and if I veered to the right, I'd go to the lodge.

Since I didn't have a reservation at the lodge, it made sense to stop by the lodge and change into my formal wear. That would be the smart thing to do.

But the truth was I didn't want to wait to see Bianca.

I wanted to see her now. These two days without her had been sheer torture. I was regretting not telling her I was leaving.

My mother had been surprisingly understanding. I think she might have been actually a bit relieved that I had finally found someone to share my life with.

After some deliberation I veered right, heading toward the lodge. I'd go in the back door so as not to be disruptive.

The minute I stepped through the back door, I heard the orchestra music. The lounge was closed, so any idea I might have had of stopping in for a burger and fries was out.

But I wasn't here for the food or the music. I was here for one purpose and one purpose only.

I was here to find Bianca.

Leaving my luggage standing at the back door, I went toward the lobby and looked around.

It hardly looked like the same place.

The tall grand Christmas tree was the same. The large four-sided fireplace in the middle of the room with flickering flames giving off cozy warmth.

Besides the five-piece orchestra playing Christmas music, the lodge was filled with elegant, formally dressed men and women standing around, champagne glasses and small plates of food. The guests completely changed the whole look of the place.

I looked carefully for Bianca, but considering that everyone had masks over their eyes, it proved to be virtually impossible.

"Hello Scott." I recognized Arabella's voice and her smile, so similar to Bianca's but about ten years older.

"Arabella," I said. "I'm looking for Bianca." No use in beating around the bush.

I knew why I was here and if other people didn't already know, they would know shortly.

"She went home to get dressed." A frown crossed her features. "Actually she should have been back an hour ago."

A little spurt of alarm shot through me. "Did she walk? Do you know?"

"I'm sure she did," Arabella said. "She thinks nothing of it."

"I'm going to look for her," I said, spinning around on my heels, not even waiting for a response.

I left my suitcase by the back door. It was the least of my concerns.

If something happened to Bianca, I would never forgive myself. I never should have left her here. At the least, I should have told her I was leaving and when I would be back.

A phone number would not have been unreasonable.

It wouldn't happen again. Lesson learned.

I didn't see any lights on in the house. Taking the front steps two at the time, I knocked on the door.

Turning around, I scanned the area as I waited. I didn't see any signs of anyone. Everyone was at their Christmas Eve party.

I knocked again, a little louder this time.

I was calm in a crisis. A pilot who panicked would find himself in a bad way in no time. It took everything I had not to pound on the door. Calling out the National Guard was sounding like a viable idea at this particular moment.

Then I heard the door unlocking.

Relief nearly took me to my knees, but I kept myself calm.

"Hi," I said when she opened the door, surprise in her bright green eyes.

She was wearing gray sweatpants and an Alpine Lodge sweatshirt. Gray with red letters and a little embroidered outline of the lodge.

Her hair was down, falling loosely around her shoulders. No makeup, just soft features and lips that beckoned to be kissed.

"Hi," she said, running a hand self-consciously through her hair.

I wanted to sweep her into my arms and never let her go.

But I didn't. Instead I put a hand on the door casing and smiled. I couldn't help it.

"What are you doing?" I asked.

"Nothing," she said as though she was surprised at her own answer.

"Nothing?"

She shrugged.

"Aren't you supposed to be at the masquerade ball?"

"Probably. Instead I'm doing nothing."

"Can I come inside? Do nothing with you?"

"Of course," she stepped back. "Come in." Glanced behind me. "It's snowing."

"It is," I said stepping inside and closing the door. "Finally."

"You got your wish," she said.

"My wish?" I followed her into the living room where she had a cozy fire going. A bottle of champagne and a full glass in a tray on the coffee table.

"At the fountain," she said, sitting down on the sofa near the fireplace and rubbing her arms. "You wished for Christmas snow."

I smiled sheepishly as I pulled off my gloves and slid out of my coat.

I remembered, now, telling her that I wished for Christmas snow. That had only been part of my wish. There was more. So much more. I decided not to clarify that. Not right now.

"You're not at the masquerade ball," I pointed out again.

She blew out a breath.

"I know. I decided it was a good night to do nothing."

"While no one is home," I said. "I get it. Your sister was a little worried about you."

"She's always worried about something. Do you want some champagne?"

"Sure. May I?"

At her nod, I headed back to the kitchen for a glass.

This was so much more than I could have wished for. Having Bianca all to myself. And on Christmas Eve as well. That was a whole lot more in line with my wish at the fountain.

Back at the sofa, I poured a small amount of champagne in my glass and held it up for a toast.

"To doing nothing," I said.

Smiling she clicked her glass against mine.

"To doing nothing."

Doing nothing with Bianca was better than doing just about anything I could think of with anyone else.

Fifty

Bianca

I hadn't been sitting on the sofa for long when someone knocked on the front door. I'd taken my time changing into comfortable clothes. Brushing out my hair. If I was going to do nothing, I wanted to do it right.

A girl didn't grow up in the Flynn family without learning how to get a good fire going in the fireplace. So I had that going.

I had just settled in on the sofa when someone showed up at the door.

When I saw that it was Scott, I was speechless. I was so thrown off guard that I forgot to ask him to come inside.

"I didn't know you were coming back," I said.

"I should have told you. I should have at least left you a note. My plan was to just run home, spend a little time with my family and come right back."

I nodded. In typical pilot language, his idea of "running home" was hopping in an airplane and flying to another state.

I should be used to such thinking.

"It's Christmas Eve," I said, pointing out the obvious.

"I told you I would never leave you at Christmas." He leaned forward. Took my hands in his. "Specifically I think I told you I wouldn't go off and visit my own family on Christmas."

I bit my lip, but couldn't hide the smile.

"You did say that. But…"

"But you didn't believe me."

"It's not that. I thought you were talking hypothetically. Besides I wasn't going to hold you to it anyway."

"Ma chérie," he said. "You should always hold me accountable for anything I tell you."

I smiled, mostly at the unexpected French endearment. Something I had not expected from him. But in ten years, he'd had lots of different experiences. Something I didn't really want to think about. Right now I just wanted to think about him being here.

With me.

On Christmas Eve.

"I'll take that under advisement," I said.

He released my hands and ran his over his slacks, staring into the flames.

My hands shaking a little, I picked up my glass and took a sip of my champagne. "You seem like something's bothering you."

"No," he said, turning his blue eyes back to mine. "I'm just relaxing. Enjoying the moment."

"You just got back?" It was more of a statement than a question.

"I might be in something of a bind. I don't even have a place to stay the night."

"You know you can stay here," I said, dismissively.

One of the logs fell in the fireplace sending sparks flying up the chimney. A wolf howled somewhere outside, reminding me that Arabella might not be completely wrong in being wary of walking the trails at night alone.

I still didn't know why he was here. Why was he here and not in Arizona with his own family?

"I 'um... I have something to tell you."

"Yeah?" His eyes lit up.

I nodded, my throat suddenly feeling closed.

"Am I supposed to guess?"

"You can guess," I said.

He put a finger against his chin.

"Let's see... you finally sent the fellow in Denver a text."

My eyes widened, then narrowed. "How did you know?"

"It was wishful thinking," he said. "So you did?"

"Yes," I said. "It was the night before you left."

"I feel like a heel."

"But your intentions were good, right?"

He took my hands again. "You have no idea."

Then he slid to the floor onto his knees.

"Scott? What? What are you—?"

"I'd been trying to think of the perfect gift to give you. On the way to Arizona I figured out what it was."

My heart was pounding dangerously and I could barely take a deep breath.

"I know this is seems sudden," he said. "But it doesn't feel sudden to me. To me it feels like it was destined from the start."

Squeezing his hands to keep myself steady, I searched his eyes.

I'd thought he was going to kiss me, but he was on his knees.

With one swift movement, he reached into his pocket and pulled out a little box.

No longer hesitant, he popped the lid open and held up a diamond solitaire engagement ring. It sparkled in the moonlight.

"Bianca," he said. "Will you marry me?"

I glanced from the ring back up to his eyes. He was serious.

This was really happening.

"But... I live... You live..."

"Yes. I know we have a lot of details to work out. But I'm thinking we can figure those things out together."

He slipped the ring out of the box. "Will you spend the rest of our lives with me? Will you be my wife?"

I nod. It was the best I could do.

"Yes?" He grinned and slid the ring on my finger.

I dropped to my knees and wrapped my arms around him.

We shifted until I was sitting on his knee.

And then he kissed me.

All the pieces of my life shifted, falling into place.

I had been waiting for him for as long as I could remember.

And the wish I'd made at the little water fountain in town had come true.

I would never again doubt the power of a wish.

Epilogue

Bianca

We bundled up in our coats and took a walk, hand in hand, back to the lodge to get Scott's luggage.

Breathing the cold air into my lungs seemed to help me regain the use of my words.

"How will this work?" I asked. "With you living in Houston?"

"Skye Travels has a location in Denver."

"Where Jackson works."

"Sure."

"But transferring to Denver could take months."

"I don't think so," he said, glancing at his watch. "I'll call Noah in the morning."

"Okay," I said. I shouldn't doubt that. Noah, the owner of Skye Travels was good to his people.

"Trust me," he said, leaning over to kiss the back of my hand.

"I trust you."

As we neared the lodge, the orchestra music spilled out through the windows and a few snowflakes fell around us.

"Are you sure you don't want to go inside?" he asked.

"I'm sure. But let's go peek in the window."

We walked across the lawn and stopped in front of the full floor-to-ceiling windows.

Couples waltzed around the lobby turned ballroom. The men in their tuxedos. The women in their ballgown. Black swirled with red and green and even flickers of white. The dance floor was like a twinkling Christmas tree. So beautiful.

It was like a dream.

But I didn't want to be in the middle of it.

I wanted to be exactly where I was. Right out here in my own little magic world with Scott.

My fiancé.

I didn't know how we would work out all the details, but he seemed confident that we would. The details didn't matter.

What mattered was that whatever happened, we would be together.

Forever and ever.

I sighed.

Scott looked over at me.

"Bianca?" he asked. "Can I have this dance?"

"Yes," I said on a little laugh.

Taking me into his arms, he pulled me into a waltz. We had our own dance floor, the lawn, all to ourselves.

Snowflakes fell around us and we were dancing together in our very own live snow globe.

After twirling me around, he took me into a dip.

And when he kissed me, I felt it all the down to my bones.

Only this time, I really was the one being kissed.

Wishes really did come true.

THE END.

Keep reading for a preview of
Finding True North...

Finding True North

Chapter 1

Andrea Flynn
December

Seatbelt. Check.

Landing gear down. Check.

Flaps down. Check.

Final approach to the Alpine Falls runway.

My first trip home flying solo.

The last time I came home, my brother Christopher had flown me here in his helicopter. It hadn't been a big deal. Just a run-of-the-mill trip he made all the time.

Not like this one.

The snowcapped mountain peaks on three sides of the vale stand tall and jagged.

The runway below looks like a postage stamp from my vantage point.

Nothing at all like the complex runways I'm accustomed to navigating.

Flying at this elevation is somewhat different from flying at lower elevations.

I keep my eyes on the computer monitors. Watching wind speed. Crosswinds.

Fortunately, it's a clear day. Nothing out of the ordinary.

Alpine Falls comes in right at ten thousand feet in elevation.

An extraordinarily high elevation for a town. And yet everyone who lives here calls the snowcapped mountains surrounding it on three sides the high country.

It typically snows here before Christmas in Alpine Falls, probably about fifty percent of the time. Maybe seventy percent.

The runway is a little tiny postage stamp surrounded by trees on all sides. A rushing mountain stream on one side. On the other side is a packed earth trail leading to the Alpine Lodge and my family's home.

The trees, maple, aspen, and pine, have all shed their leaves since the last time I was here, but the blue spruce trees still have their needles. The blue spruce trees look like a grove of undecorated Christmas trees, which I suppose in some ways, they really are.

This is apparently one of those years when the snow

doesn't fall before Christmas. I see no signs of snow on the ground as I take the little Cessna in for a landing.

This isn't one of the usual airplanes I fly. In fact, it isn't even a Skye Travels airplane. It's one of my boss's private planes that he'd generously allowed me to borrow for the week.

Those few seconds of ground effect before the airplane wheels hit the runway are the one time when the airplane actually feels like it's floating. Maybe it's just me.

Probably just me since technically it's floating the whole time it's in the air.

My wheels bump against the runway and the plane slows to a stop. I taxi around to one of the areas designated for parking. There is no terminal. No building at all. The runway has nothing more than two air socks. Three would be better for crosswind detection.

I proceed to go through the usual post-flight checklist.

I check my watch. I've landed thirty minutes earlier than I had anticipated.

Not that I expect a lot of fanfare for my first solo flight home. However. With five brothers and sisters, four of them married, it seems a bit to me like someone would have shown up to meet me and to witness my first landing at the Alpine Falls runway. Such that it is.

Literally just a runway.

There's no one here.

But I'm early.

I secure the airplane and open the door.

The cold wind, even though I grew up with it, catches me off-guard as it slaps me in the face.

I grab my coat on the seat next to me and shrug into it, buttoning it up. I didn't bring gloves or a hat, but we always have extra at the house.

With my coat on now, I climb out of the airplane and open up the cargo area.

Unlike my sisters, I have learned to travel light. I'm home for a week with just one small suitcase.

I double-check to make sure I have everything. My phone case strapped over my shoulders. The airplane locked. My luggage.

With everything I need, I start down the path leading home.

Even though I currently live in Denver, Alpine Falls will always be the place I think of as home.

Being the youngest of six siblings, three of whom still live in Alpine Falls along with our parents, there is always someone in the family around.

Unless, of course, I'm wanting to show off my landing skills.

The air is a lot lighter than I'm used to and I can feel my skin drying out already.

I'm prepared. I have lots of moisturizer in my luggage. That's something I never forget.

Dragging my suitcase behind me, I turn left at a fork in the path. The path to the right leads to the Alpine Lodge. My family owns the lodge and my oldest sister, Arabella, runs it as the official manager. But it's a family business and everyone chips in when they're around. I'll be given some task or another, too, while I'm here. I don't mind. It's expected. We all grew up working at the lodge.

I'm especially looking forward to seeing my brother Jackson. Jackson, like me, is a private pilot.

And Jackson, like me, works for Skye Travels. I work in Denver, though, and he works in the Houston office.

I still have hope that we'll someday at least work in the same city, but that would probably require me to move to Houston.

The Skye Travels home office is based in Houston where it was started by Noah Worthington and that's where most of the company's airplanes are housed.

Noah founded Skye Travels with just one little Cessna airplane and a whole lot of legendary customer service.

Now he owns and operates the largest private airline company in the country. Like Alpine Lodge, Skye Travels is family owned and operated. So much so that all things being equal, he'll hire his family first. To his credit, even though he boldly embraces nepotism, he makes sure that anyone he hires, especially his family, even more so, is the most qualified person for the job.

My brother and I were lucky to get hired on with Skye Travels. The competition is steep.

A little chipmunk runs up in front of me, stands on his hind legs, then realizing I'm not going to feed him, takes off just as fast.

The chipmunks always make me smile.

I follow the path to the back door of the house and walk in through the unlocked door.

I roll my eyes. This would never happen on purpose in Denver. After living away from Alpine Falls, first for college, then for work, I don't think I can ever go back to feeling comfortable leaving my door unlocked.

Too much can happen.

And the lodge is just a quick walk away. More people means more opportunities to have someone wander in.

I automatically take off my coat and hang it on one of pegs near the back door before going into the kitchen.

Tabitha, sitting at the breakfast table, looks up. Tabitha is my oldest brother's wife. Moose, her big solid white husky stands up and wags his tail.

"Andrea," she says with a glance at her watch. "You're early."

Tabitha has Christmas wrapping paper, ribbons, and boxes spread all over the table.

"A little," I say, pleased that someone at least noticed that I was early. I run my hands over Moose's head and he licks me affectionately.

"I was planning on walking down to meet you at the airport."

Tabitha, bless her heart, was still calling the runway an airport.

"It's okay."

She stands up and puts both hands on her very huge, very pregnant stomach and stretches her back.

"How are you feeling?" I ask. She can't possibly be feeling like walking anywhere.

"I feel good," she says, smiling. "I'm big as a house, huh?"

She must have seen my shocked expression. I force myself to smile back.

"A little bigger than the last time I saw you." I glance around. "Where is everybody else?" Surely she didn't need to be here alone.

"Here and there. Your mother is upstairs getting the guest room ready."

"Guest room?" Most guests took rooms over at the lodge. That's what it was for after all. Only special friends of the family stayed in one of our guest rooms here at our house.

"Jackson's bringing a friend home for the week."

"Oh." I'd been looking forward to catching up with Jackson, but if he was bringing a girlfriend, then I could forget spending any quality time with him.

I obviously hadn't brought a boyfriend. It had been about six months since I'd even gone out with anyone and from the looks of what was available out there in the dating world, I was better off by far being single.

"Can I get you anything before I take my things upstairs?"

Tabitha bites her lip. "I was going to ask if I could get you anything."

I've always liked Tabitha. She has a huge heart and a generous spirit.

"Let me get settled in and I'll come back down for some hot tea. You can drink tea, right?"

Tabitha grins. "Sure can. I'll get everything ready."

Knowing I'm fighting a losing battle on keeping her from doing anything for me, I agree and head upstairs to my room.

The big house rambles. That's the best way to describe it. I walk through the foyer, past the old grandfather clock that punctuates the minutes and head upstairs.

The house started out as what most people would call a normal house. But now, even though it has eight bedrooms and nine bathrooms on three different floors, there is never any crowded feeling. Not even when we're all here together.

Technically, it isn't just a house. It's what most people called a mansion. I personally call it a manor, even though everyone tends to think that title a bit too European.

The nearby lodge, Alpine Lodge, had actually been built before the house. The lodge has been in the family since my great-great grandparents claimed the land and proceeded to grow their family of twelve children.

After their children (nine daughters) left home, they had begun renting out the many vacant rooms. That was how the lodge was born.

Their son, my great grandfather had married and together he and his wife had built the house that my family now lives in. They, too, had a large family and although they had started off with a normal sized house, each generation built on more rooms over the years. Each generation, it seemed, added one touch or another to the house. The effect was a large rambling house with plenty of room for extended family.

Even when I had lived here with two married brothers and one married sister, we all never stepped on each other's toes. It was only after people visited our house that they understood how adult children could live with their parents and it not be weird.

Our parents had their own two-story suite of rooms and their own entrance to the outside.

The house was that big and rambling.

The kitchen was one part of the house that we all shared. The kitchen, breakfast room, and the dining room.

My room, on the second floor, still carries a vibe from my teenage years. I took down all the rock star posters before I left home, but my trophies and books still fill a bookcase along one wall.

I open up my suitcase and quickly hang my clothes in the closet. As a pilot, I learned to travel with all my clothes on hangers. Saves countless time and energy.

I change out of my pilot's uniform into a pair of jeans and a gray Alpine Falls sweatshirt.

After washing my face and giving my hair a quick brushing, I pull it back in a messy ponytail. Good enough.

After Jackson gets here, I'll probably go over to the lodge. Check out the Christmas decorations. My sister, Arabella will doubtlessly put me to work, but I'll take the book I'm reading with me just in case I have time to relax in front of the big stone fireplace.

Leaving my room, I see my mother coming from the guest room down the hall.

"There's my favorite daughter," she says, pulling me into a big hug.

Of course I know I'm not her favorite daughter. She tells all of us that. Besides, we all know that Christopher, the oldest, is her favorite child.

It became especially obvious when she talked Daddy into building a helipad near the runway in order to lure him back to Alpine Falls. How could we not notice?

"I heard Jackson is bringing a friend home," I say as we walk side by side toward the stairs. "Have we met her before?"

"I didn't even ask," Mama says. "He just asked if the guest room was available." She glances over at me with a sideways glance. "I should have asked you if you were bringing anyone."

"I would have told you," I say, biting back a sigh. "but no. Not this year."

"You know," she says, locking an arm with mine. "You're not getting any younger."

"Momma." I roll my eyes. "You've got Tabitha just about ready to pop. You shouldn't be worried about me getting married."

"Just because you're the youngest doesn't mean you shouldn't be thinking about getting married and settling down."

I take a deep breath. "I will take that opinion under advisement," I say. "But it's not like it was when you were growing up. People, especially career people, wait until they're in their thirties to get married."

Now Momma rolls her eyes.

"You have no idea how quickly time flies. Just don't wait too long."

"Yes. Momma."

"You and Jackson might as well be twins."

"You're so very lucky to have two of us."

As we walk down the stairs, I wonder what's come over my mother. She hardly ever gives me a hard time about settling down.

Probably something in the air.

Maybe it has something to do with it being Christmas.

Christmas puts everyone in a different kind of mood.

As for me, I had no intention of settling down anytime soon and I had every intent of spending this Christmas without the complications of a boyfriend.

Finding True North

PREVIEW

Chapter 2
Daniel Worthington

It's my first time to the little town of Alpine Falls.

"Prepare for landing," Jackson Flynn says into the headset.

Habit. It's just habit. We're the only two in the airplane. Jackson is in the pilot's seat and I'm in the copilot's seat.

I look out the window at the little town unfolding below. It's more like a community, really, than a town. Born and raised in Houston, I'm a big city guy. Nonetheless, I've flown into my share of small towns.

Jackson takes the plane down toward the runway.

The familiar sound of the wheels going down. The flaps

down. The chatter from the nearby Glenwood Springs airport.

Jackson and I both work as pilots for Skye Travels. Hired at the same time, we'd bonded during orientation three years ago.

"Are you sure your family won't mind me intruding on their Christmas?"

"I promise it's not an intrusion. We're a big family. I doubt they'll even notice you're here."

"I'm going to take that in the best possible way," I say.

"As you should."

My parents had decided to jet off to Switzerland for Christmas this year to celebrate their recent retirement. They were calling it a second honeymoon. I think that was their way of not inviting me.

As such I hadn't made any plans for Christmas. It wasn't a big deal if I ended up spending it alone. I wasn't a scrooge, but being an only child, I was used to quiet holidays.

Jackson, however, wouldn't have it. He insisted on me joining his family in Alpine Falls.

I had to admit I was curious. I'd never spent Christmas in a small town or with a large family. It promised to be an interesting week.

Our wheels touch the runway and I notice another airplane already parked. As to be expected in a small town, there is no terminal. Just a couple of air socks.

"Someone's already here," I say as he taxies over to park next to the little Cessna.

"I don't recognize that airplane," Jackson says.

"It's not one of ours," I say, stating the obvious since there is no Skye Travels logo splashed across it. "Probably belongs to a guest."

"Probably." A quick Internet search of Alpine Lodge had told me it was an old, but elegant lodge. A Christmas destination for many.

Apparently people come here year after year to spend their Christmas holiday at the lodge.

My phone chimes with a text message.

"Anything important?" Jackson asked.

"Sophia."

"I thought you two broke up."

I thought so, too," I say, putting my phone away without reading the message.

"Hasn't snowed yet," Jackson says as he goes through the post flight checklist.

"Is that unusual?"

He shrugs. "Somewhat." He glances toward the rugged mountain peaks with white clouds clustering around them. "It'll snow sometime this week."

Snow wasn't in the forecast, but since Jackson had grown up here, I'd take his forecast over the meteorologists' any day.

"I hope so," I say. "A white Christmas will be a new experience."

"I feel sorry for you," Jackson says.

"Do we have transportation coming?" I ask, changing the subject.

"We walk," Jackson says.

I raise an eyebrow. This is most definitely going to be a different experience. Different from any other Christmas I've ever had.

A Christmas to remember.

We put on our coats, climb out of the airplane, and pull our suitcases out of the cargo hold.

Jackson had not been kidding. Our transportation consisted of walking.

Rolling our suitcases behind us, we follow the packed dirt trail from the runway into the trees.

"It's pretty here," I say as we walk through a grove of blue spruce trees.

"You should see it in the fall before the maple and aspen trees shed their leaves."

"I can imagine. I haven't spent much time in this part of the country."

"It gets into your blood," Jackson says.

We turn left at a fork in the path.

"Go that way," Jackson says. "to get to the lodge. Then keep going to get to town."

"Got it." I pull my collar up over my ears to keep the bitingly cold wind from killing my ears.

We go in through the back door of what looks like a big rambling house. An old house, but well maintained.

Three women sit at the kitchen table drinking from coffee cups.

"There's my favorite son," the older woman pulls Jackson into a hug.

"She says that to all of us," Jackson says. "This is my

mother." He turns to the other women. "My very pregnant sister-in-law, Tabitha, and my sister."

"It's a pleasure to meet you Mrs. Flynn," I say. "I've heard nothing but good things about you.

My gaze touches his sister-in-law, then slides to his sister and freezes.

Chapter 3
Andrea

I breathe in the steam wafting out of the mug of hot tea, then take a little sip. The green tea has enough honey to make it palatable. Personally I would prefer a cup of coffee—with enough cream to kill the taste—but since Tabitha isn't supposed to have caffeine, I don't want to be rude and drink coffee in front of her.

Momma and Tabitha are talking about baby things and my attention wanders. Moose comes over and puts his head in my lap, seemingly just as bored with listening to talk of babies as I am.

I rub his soft fur and think about getting a dog for myself. Of course I know I won't do it. I can't.

As a pilot I'm not home enough to take care of a pet. So I have to enjoy my sister-in-law's dog when I'm here.

The back door opens and I hear muffled voices as a couple of guys come inside and hang their coats on a peg by the door. I recognize Jackson's voice as one of them.

I glance up just in time to see my brother walking into the kitchen. My mother gives him a hug, then Jackson introduces us.

I look past my brother, fully expecting to see his latest girlfriend, but instead my gaze locks onto a handsome man about my brother's age, wearing the same pilot's uniform as Jackson. The same Skye Travels embroidered emblem. The same one on my shirts and jackets and cap.

When his gaze meets mine, he doesn't look away. Instead his lips turn up into a slow smile that scatters my heart rate and lets loose a bevy of butterflies in my stomach.

"This is Daniel," my brother's words register somehow in my brain despite the sudden disappearance of all my sense.

I work with pilots all day long every day. Meeting someone new who happens to be a pilot is not something new or unusual for me. It's just an everyday run of the mill occurrence.

Meeting a pilot who has a visceral effect on me, however, is anything but an everyday run of the mill occurrence.

"I'm going to show Daniel to his room," Jackson says.

"Come back down after you get two get settled," Momma says. "I'll make a pot of coffee."

Coffee. What a wonderful idea.

After Jackson and Daniel leave the kitchen, I realize I'm still holding my cup of tea out in front of me in both hands. Nothing has moved other than my eyes.

Tabitha glances over at me.

"Are you okay?" she asks.

No. "Yes." I set the mug down. "I think I'll have some coffee, too."

Momma is already measuring coffee into the fancy machine someone had brought home last year. I think it had been my brother Reed or maybe it had been Christopher. Definitely one of my brothers.

After I take a sip of tea and set the mug down, I realize my hands are trembling.

I clear my throat and straighten.

"I thought Jackson was bringing home a girl," Tabitha says.

"I think we all just assumed it," Momma said, sitting back down at the breakfast table. "I guess not."

Tabitha glances over at me. I'm keeping my gaze focused on the tea in my mug.

"He's kinda cute," she says in what is obviously intended as a little whisper.

"I hadn't noticed," I say.

I almost miss the glance exchanged between Momma and Tabitha before they go back to talking about cribs and high chairs.

Anyone with any sense at all would know that I was lying. Anybody who took one look at Daniel could see that he was not only kinda cute, he was drop dead gorgeous.

The kind of handsome man that no doubt had women falling at his feet.

And with that slow grin of his, he obviously knows it.

There is nothing more dangerous to a woman's heart than a handsome pilot in uniform.

Coming from a family of pilots AND working with pilots every day, I've been inoculated.

Handsome pilots don't have an effect on me.

Until they do.

Finding True North

PREVIEW

Chapter 4
Daniel

I follow Jackson from the kitchen, through an open foyer, and up a flight of stairs.

The old house is bigger than it looked like from the outside and it rambles.

"The guest room is right in here," Jackson says, opening the door to a room down a short hallway after turning left at the top of the stairs.

The guest room isn't exactly what I had expected. It looks like it was designed specifically to be a guest room, not just a room with a bed thrown in it or left in it as the case may be which what my parents had done to my room after I left home. My old bedroom was now my mother's craft room with a bed in it.

Besides the bed, there is a nightstand with a lamp and a phone charger. A little computer desk and chair against one wall. Besides the obvious conveniences, it's the view from the large window that instantly draws my attention.

From the window I have an unparalleled view of a meadow stretching to the feet of the tall rugged mountain peaks. The snow-capped mountains have white clouds clustered around them. They look different, already, than they had as we had landed at the runway.

Snowing. That's what Jackson tells me. It's snowing in what he calls the high country.

"Nice view," I say.

"Be careful," Jackson says. "It's easy to get used to."

I turn around and look at him.

He has a rather odd expression on his face and I wonder if we're actually talking about the view.

But then he claps me on the shoulder.

"Let me know if you need anything," he says. "Come on downstairs for coffee when you're ready."

"Will do."

I turn back to the view and realize that it's Jackson's sister that I'm thinking about. She looks a little like Jackson. Same dark hair, hers tumbling around her shoulders. Same eyes except hers are sparkling green. And those lips. Most definitely kissable lips.

He hadn't even told me her name.

All I knew about her is that she's Jackson's sister.

And, oddly enough, that's more than I need to know.

With just one glance I knew that my life as a confirmed bachelor teetered on the edge of being over.

That thought reminds me to check my messages.

SOPHIA

Are we still getting together for Christmas?

I stare at the message. Sophia and I had broken up two weeks ago. I was pretty sure we had left that in no uncertain terms.

Maybe this is one of those messages that somehow got caught up in cyberspace and only just now landed in my phone.

With all the flying that I do, my phone sometimes gets its wires crossed.

So I ignore the message.

There's no reason to respond to it and embarrass her. Just because we had broken up, doesn't mean I want to embarrass her by answering a text that she sent weeks ago.

I open up my suitcase and hang my clothes on a cast iron rod attached to the wall. An interesting design. Perfect for a guest room.

After washing my face and running a comb through my hair, I change into jeans and a long-sleeve shirt. Should have brought some heavier clothes. Unfortunately I don't own any.

Sounds like I need to take a walk into town. Surely they have a shop that sells sweatshirts.

I put on my boots, lace them up, and deem myself ready to go downstairs for coffee.

It's time to find out more about Jackson's sister.

My friend has been holding out on me. He told me he came from a big family and had sisters, but he didn't tell me he had a beautiful goddess sister.

Keep Reading
Finding True North at Alpine Falls...

Get your copy at www.kathrynkaleigh.com

ALPINE FALLS

DON'T MISS ANY OF THE
SILVER PINES SECOND CHANCES
SERIES:

www.kathrynkaleigh.com

No matter how many years passed...
They never forgot...
And their love never dimmed.

A ghostly presence...
A rip in time that never healed...
An impossible romance...

Sign up for my NEWSLETTER to get all my romance releases, sales, Kickstarter announcements, and a **FREE** romance, SEALED WITH A KISS